DEAD AS DEAD

Stubbins lay on the floor with the rat droppings, dead as a fried carp. Fargo kicked him to make certain, then kicked him again to make *absolutely* certain, and only then did he holster his weapon.

When he turned the body over, he found that his first bullet had gone straight through Stubbins' heart, and the second had gone through his belly.

He gave the body another kick, then grabbed the corpse's arm and dragged it outside through the tunnel. One more to toss on the pile.

He did, and after he did, he glared at the corpse, saying, "Now stay dead this time, or else!"

THE
TRAILSMAN
#326

SILVER
MOUNTAIN
SLAUGHTER

by

Jon Sharpe

A SIGNET BOOK

SIGNET
Published by New American Library, a division of
Penguin Group (USA) Inc., 375 Hudson Street,
New York, New York 10014, USA
Penguin Group (Canada), 90 Eglinton Avenue East, Suite 700, Toronto,
Ontario M4P 2Y3, Canada (a division of Pearson Penguin Canada Inc.)
Penguin Books Ltd., 80 Strand, London WC2R 0RL, England
Penguin Ireland, 25 St. Stephen's Green, Dublin 2,
Ireland (a division of Penguin Books Ltd.)
Penguin Group (Australia), 250 Camberwell Road, Camberwell, Victoria 3124,
Australia (a division of Pearson Australia Group Pty. Ltd.)
Penguin Books India Pvt. Ltd., 11 Community Centre, Panchsheel Park,
New Delhi - 110 017, India
Penguin Group (NZ), 67 Apollo Drive, Rosedale, North Shore 0632,
New Zealand (a division of Pearson New Zealand Ltd.)
Penguin Books (South Africa) (Pty.) Ltd., 24 Sturdee Avenue,
Rosebank, Johannesburg 2196, South Africa

Penguin Books Ltd., Registered Offices:
80 Strand, London WC2R 0RL, England

First published by Signet, an imprint of New American Library,
a division of Penguin Group (USA) Inc.

First Printing, December 2008
10 9 8 7 6 5 4 3 2 1

The first chapter of this book previously appeared in *Seminole Showdown*,
the three hundred twenty-fifth volume in this series.

The Trailsman

Beginnings . . . they bend the tree and they mark the man. Skye Fargo was born when he was eighteen. Terror was his midwife, vengeance his first cry. Killing spawned Skye Fargo, ruthless, cold-blooded murder. Out of the acrid smoke of gunpowder still hanging in the air, he rose, cried out a promise never forgotten.

The Trailsman they began to call him all across the West: searcher, scout, hunter, the man who could see where others only looked, his skills for hire but not his soul, the man who lived each day to the fullest, yet trailed each tomorrow. Skye Fargo, the Trailsman, the seeker who could take the wildness of a land and the wanting of a woman and make them his own.

*Arizona, 1861—in the heat of the desert,
amid the cacti and the sagebrush,
only one thing burns hotter than the sun above—
the Trailsman's fury.*

1

Winter in the high country had been hard, about as hard as the Trailsman could remember. He'd spent the better part of it high up in the California Rockies in an old trapper's cabin. When he wasn't huddled against the bone-numbing cold and its accompanying biting wind, he'd split most of his time between gathering what wood he could find that was fit to feed his fire, and trying to persuade his horse, the Ovaro, not to climb directly into it to keep warm.

At winter's end, the tall man and his trusty black-and-white paint stallion had emerged relatively safe and sound, if a little on the gaunt side, and had headed southeast: a path that took them down toward the Arizona Territory and its promise of sunshine and warmth.

Well, he was sure as hell reaping that promise now, he thought in exasperation as he rode the flat, desolate stretch of desert between Phoenix and Tucson. It had been eighty degrees when he woke at just past dawn, and now, at midmorning, he was sweating up a storm and cursing his buckskins. He would have been smarter to make himself a buckskin loincloth!

Suddenly, he reined the Ovaro to a halt, slithered down out of the saddle, and began to tug off his shirt. When it finally loosed its damp hold on his skin and he peeled it off, overhead, the breeze tickling his skin felt like a miracle.

"Better," he hissed between clenched teeth as he cinched his shirt across the back of his saddle, then secured it with the tie-down latigos.

He knew it was stupid to ride without a shirt this time of year, but right at the moment, the pain of a future sunburn was nothing compared to the here-and-now hellish steam bath of riding inside that leather shirt.

He swung up onto the Ovaro and nudged the stud into a slow jog, the breeze tickling his long-suffering skin. *Yes,* he thought, *much better.*

And then he noticed it.

Just a dot on the horizon, a dot growing larger and separating into tiny black figures as he drew nearer. *Bandidos?* Pilgrims? A million possibilities tumbled through his mind as he rode closer. Not hostile Indians, he decided early on. At least, as soon as it became apparent that one of the objects ahead was a buckboard, which was definitely not an Apache affectation.

But something about the rig—and the folks traveling with it—seemed somehow wrong. For one thing, the fellow in the driver's seat wore a tall stovepipe hat with a turkey feather sprouting from its hatband. He also wore a bright yellow vest, the sort in which you might expect to see some New Orleans cardsharp attired. But not an Arizona pilgrim, or a miner, or a cattle or horse rancher. It was the wrong sort of picture.

Beside the odd duck driving the team sat what looked like a young girl. Maybe twenty or so, Fargo thought. But that was probably just wishful thinking. It had been a few months since he'd set his eyes on a girl worth looking at.

"Don't start getting yourself bothered," he muttered so that only the Ovaro heard. "She's probably some old Hopi squaw."

Still, he pushed the Ovaro into a speedier jog.

Although it seemed forever, he caught up with them in no time, and the rig's driver didn't seem surprised to see him. "Took you a while," the old man said, turning slightly in his seat. Protruding from the outlandish hat was a scant series of long white wisps that the Trailsman hadn't seen from afar, and the man seemed to have only a quarter of his original complement of teeth. Those that remained were stained by tobacco.

The girl didn't look at either one of them. She just kept the same posture she'd held since he first made her out—slumped forward, eyes on her hands in her lap. He couldn't see her face, but he took some comfort in the fact that her hands didn't look old and gnarled.

Fargo turned his attention back to the wagon's driver. "You a pilgrim?" he asked, more as an excuse to keep pace with the rig than out of any real curiosity.

The old man jutted a skeletal hand out toward him. "Franklin Q. Stubbins, at yer service."

The Trailsman took it and gave it a shake. "Skye Fargo's my name," he said. "Most folks know me as the Trailsman."

"I will, too, then," said Franklin Q. Stubbins. He then broke out into a quick but loud bray of laughter. The girl beside him didn't shift so much as half an inch.

"What you doing out here in the nowheres, Mr. Stubbins?" Fargo asked. "You on your way to Tucson?"

Again, the old man broke out into that peculiar bray of laughter. "Mebbe, mebbe," he replied. "We'll see how the water holds out."

3

The Trailsman's brow wrinkled. Just what did the crazy old coot mean by that? He looked over at the girl again. She had cringed down into herself at Stubbins' last comment, and Fargo was beginning to wonder how they had paired up. And if she was as crazy as Stubbins was. She'd have to be either crazy or desperate to share a buckboard seat with him all the way down to Tucson.

So he simply nodded, as if the old man's comment about the water made perfect sense to him, and asked, "Where do you and your daughter plan to bide? I've heard good things about the Wigwam Hotel."

His little stab at finding out about the girl bore fruit sooner than he'd hoped, because Stubbins immediately replied, "Oh, she ain't my daughter, no, not by a long shot. Been a few years since I had the itch so bad I'd scratch it with a squaw." And then came that laugh again.

"Not your wife, either?" Fargo asked.

"Hell, no," Stubbins said. And then he punched the girl in the arm hard enough to merely knock her from her perch. "Speak up, gal," he said. "Tell the Trailsman here your name!"

Fargo had nearly jumped from his horse to the buckboard's seat when Stubbins struck the girl, but she suddenly wheeled toward him and he forgot all his good intentions.

She was striking. Her features bore the high cheekbones and faraway—but at the same time, intense—look of an Indian, yet her skin was not the copper or latigo color he'd expected. It was pale, almost milky, and blue eyes burned out of her face, burned him to his core.

"I am Kathleen Dugan," she said in a monotone, then turned her face from him once again.

It was a good thing she had, as the shock of her had almost made him lose his seat. While he pulled himself together again, Stubbins added, "Her pa was from County Cork, and her ma was an Apache squaw. They was neighbors to me. Her ma died and her pa went broke, and he sold her into servitude. Got her papers right here." He patted his vest pocket. "I'm havin' me some financial wear and tear of late, and that's why we're headed for Tucson. Gonna try and sell her."

Fargo barely let the last words come out of Stubbins' mouth before he asked, far too eagerly, "How much?" He knew the Tucson he was used to was chock-full of rowdies and scofflaws who'd think nothing of buying the girl, then renting her out for a nickel an hour. Or worse. All that he wanted at this moment was to permanently sever the bond between Stubbins and the fair Kathleen Dugan. The girl wouldn't even look at him for more than a second, and had said no more than four words to him in the entirety of their acquaintance. If you could call it that.

Thoughtfully, Stubbins scratched his chin between thumb and forefinger. "I'd hoped to get me a biddin' war goin'," he said. "Hoped to get enough to buy me a couple of weanling hogs and a calf. And some grain. And mayhap a fair saddle horse." He kept on scratching his chin and gazed out over the horizon.

Fargo felt himself reaching for his pocket. Well, dammit, there were some things a man just had to do.

He opened his coin purse and rooted around for the two double eagles he had put away last fall, in case of dire emergency. This was one, all right.

"Forty bucks," he said, holding the money out so that Stubbins could see but not reach it. "Final offer."

Stubbins hesitated and Fargo let him stew for a moment before he started to draw his hand back.

"Hold on there, son!" Stubbins blurted out. "I'm thinkin'!"

Fargo let his hand drop to rest on his leg while the

5

buckboard and the Ovaro moved them down through the desert. If the girl had any feelings about the transaction or her impending sale, she didn't make them known. She hadn't even looked at him, not once, save when she'd said her name at Stubbins' command.

Fargo asked, "Can she say anything besides her name? You ain't tryin' to gyp me with a one-trick pony, are you?" In truth, he had sort of been hoping that she'd be a fair conversationalist, seeing as they were going to ride down to Tucson together.

He figured to cut her free once they got there, but talking was the only thing he figured to be able to do with her till they made town. And that was another sixty miles or so.

Suddenly, he was having conflicting thoughts about her, and her freedom, and without thinking, began to draw his money-holding hand back toward his pocket.

Stubbins must have had great peripheral vision, because he suddenly snapped, "She can recite the whole Bible, almost. And I reckon forty dollars would do it, son."

This time, the laugh that followed was less a bray than a cackle. It plucked at Fargo's spine like icy fingers.

It had about the same effect on the girl, because he saw her curl in on herself. Suddenly, he didn't have any doubts anymore.

Fargo, finding the transaction more and more distasteful with each passing second, once again held the coins out toward the old geezer, stopping an inch short of where the old man could grab them. Stubbins made a face and opened his mouth, but Fargo beat him to the punch. "You said she's got transfer papers?" he asked.

"Sure, sure, she does," Stubbins croaked, and dug a grimy sheet, folded several ways, from his pocket. He waved it at Fargo. "Got 'em right here."

"Well, sign her over," Fargo said, and leaned forward to let Stubbins take the money. He sat his horse while Stubbins dug out his pencil and made his mark on the tired sheet.

Stubbins folded the paper back the way it had been while he said, "Get down, girl. You been bought." As he handed the paper up to Fargo, the girl jackrabbited off the other side of the wagon and landed about ten feet away from the buckboard. She stood there, head bent toward the ground, her arms circling her torso, her hair hanging in her eyes.

Fargo took the sheet and unfolded it, quickly scanning the spidery scrawl before he refolded it and stuck it into his back pocket. The girl was his. At least, on paper. She continued to stare at her feet.

He had expected more. Maybe a thank-you.

Stubbins tossed a ratty carpetbag to the ground, then clucked to his mule and continued on his way without another word to either of them, leaving Fargo and the girl to stare at each other. Or not. He was staring at her, but she was still focused on her shoes, which he'd just noticed were grimy moccasins.

He took her in. At least, as much as she was letting him see. She wore a faded red calico skirt that fell over long, slim legs and softly belled hips, and her blouse was white and very loose, in the Mexican peasant style.

Stubbins and his rig had nearly disappeared from sight before Fargo had the presence of mind to say, "Miss? Miss, you want to climb up behind? It's a long way to Tucson, and I don't want you travelin' on foot."

Finally, she looked up at him, turned that beautiful face toward him. In a voice that was soft but devoid of expression, she said, "Screw you, white dog."

Fargo didn't know how to react, so he just stared at her as if someone from afar was remotely operating her mouth and voice. But she'd said it nonetheless and eventually he had to say the word that had balled up in his mouth. Which, unfortunately, was, "Huh?"

"You heard me," came her reply.

She wasn't looking at him any longer, but he could guess her expression by the tone of her voice, which had grown decidedly more hostile since Stubbins had moved on down the road.

By now, he and his rig were little more than a dark, smudgy speck in the sun-blasted distance.

Fargo didn't answer her, just kept on staring at Stubbins' tiny, disappearing form to the south. But finally he said, "Get up," and reined the Ovaro in front of her.

She looked up at him, hate suddenly pasted across that beautiful, fair face, and grunted up an ugly sound.

Fargo didn't like the tone of it, not one bit, but he slid his boot from the stirrup and said, "Now."

Apparently he said it sternly enough that it had effect, because suddenly she slipped up behind his saddle and planted her fanny firmly on the Ovaro's croup.

Fargo was about to welcome her aboard when, from behind him, came her words.

"Well? Didn't you want to take me someplace? Get on with it! Or are we just going to sit here all day?"

Jaw clenched, he gave the Ovaro a little knee, and as the horse moved them forward, muttered, "Buddy, the next time you see me wantin' to do some good, or to do the right thing, just kick me right square in my bleedin' backside."

2

Fargo covered another nine or ten miles before he stopped for the day. He could have gone on another two or three miles, but he figured that a double load was harder on the Ovaro. Plus, he found an unexpected grove of mesquite trees out in the dead center of nowhere, and thought he'd best take advantage of them.

Still, he rode around and over the site for a few minutes before he reined in his horse and slid one foot free of its stirrup.

"Don't know where your friend went, but he surely didn't come through here," he said, thumbing his hat back. Neither had any Indians in the past few weeks. The ground was free of tracks, and dust lay heavy on the foliage.

The girl hit the ground almost noiselessly and said, almost too softly for Fargo to hear, "He's no friend of mine."

He blinked, but held his peace. What had he gotten himself into? And just what kind of crazy arrangement did these two have? He knew better than to ask her, though, and simply hopped down to the ground and started to strip the paint of his tack.

The girl walked off a few feet, into the deepest part of the blue shade of a mesquite, and sat down in a little cross-legged heap. She didn't say another word, which was fine with him. For the moment, all his attention was on his horse.

After the Ovaro was stripped of tack, brushed, fed, watered, and tethered between two big mesquites, Fargo's attention turned toward his own supper. This appeared to be presenting itself in the form of a covey of quail not twenty yards away. He stood a moment as they fluttered on the ground, and felt himself begin to salivate.

He slipped his rifle from its boot and held it up to his shoulder, seating it calmly as he steadied his aim through the sites. And just as he was about to pull the trigger, he caught motion at the corner of his eye and heard the girl shout, "No!"

The quail all blurred upward with a frantic flurry of beating wing strokes, and he dropped his rifle to his side. "Just what the hell is wrong with you?" he demanded. It took him a moment to realize that she was shaking. Not that he cared very much by this time. But still, curiosity was his downfall. He repeated, "What?!"

He watched her expression slowly shift. She blinked. "Don't kill them. They're spirit birds." There was a pleading quality in her voice, but it was very faint.

Flatly, he repeated, "Spirit birds?"

Her head tipped toward him and she softly snorted through her nose. "You know what I mean." And then she sat down again with a soft plop.

"Oh, hell," Fargo muttered as he shoved his rifle back into its boot. "Whatever you say, your ladyship." He swung up the saddle pack that held food and angrily began to carry it toward her. But by the time he reached her, she wasn't looking toward him any longer. He nudged her knee with his boot toe. "Get to work, princess," he said. "Gather wood for a fire."

Without a word, she rose and began searching the

weeds for kindling. He crouched and began digging through the grub sack. He pulled out the butt end of a ham that had been awfully small to begin with, and set it aside. Frankly, he was sick to death of it, but if his silent female riding companion was going to scare off all the good, live game, she'd have to make do, too. With a shake of his head, he muttered, "Good conversation, my aunt Fanny . . ."

Eventually, he got supper organized. She brought in a good armload of wood and he got a fair fire going under their supper. Amazingly, she wolfed it down like she hadn't seen full rations since Christmas last. Everything—ham, potatoes, beans, even the last piece-of-crap slice of week-old bread—went down her throat with gusto.

Toward the end, he wasn't eating anything himself, just sitting back and watching her, his mouth agape.

At last she stopped—or rather, they ran out of food—and she sat back, spine against a rock and sated, staring out into the twilight. And again, he was taken by her beauty.

"Get enough?" he asked, his throat thick. They were the first words either had spoken since she dumped the firewood at his feet, and they came out a little more, well, desirous, than he would have liked.

She didn't answer, really. Instead, she pointed her finger toward the southwest and asked, "What are those?"

He turned to look. They weren't the Santa Ritas. Those were more straight south. The only hills he could see, silhouetted by the setting sun, were low and rolling, and quite a way off in the distance.

"The Sand Hills, I reckon," he said, shrugging his shoulders. There was nothing over there. Not even a town.

She nodded, as if to signify she'd heard his reply, then fell to staring at the ground once again.

He worked at his lower lip for a while, then said, "You know, you keep starin' at the ground like that, we're gonna pass another whole day without saying a word. You want that?"

He sure didn't.

She raised that pretty head. "What do you wish to talk about?"

Encouraged by the fact that she hadn't added "White Dog" to the statement, he replied, "Anything. Your choice."

She said, "Then I choose not to speak," and twisted away to stare off in the distance.

Mouthing the phrase "Dad-blast your hide!" he moved around the campfire and sat directly in front of her. She had to look at him now. Which, in fact, she did.

"What you choose," he said, "has very little to do with it. I bought your papers. Doesn't that give me a right to a little conversation?"

She crossed her arms over a full bosom. "Then suggest a topic."

He shrugged. "Tell me about yourself. Tell me what you were like when you were a kid. Tell me what it was like livin' with ol' Stubbins." Still, she just stared, so he added, "Tell me about the first time you ever rode a horse, or the first time you went to town, or the last time Stubbins sold you."

She jerked just a tad at the last phrase, and he knew he'd hit a hot key.

He added, "He's done this before, hasn't he? Sold you off, then somehow got you back."

She wasn't looking up at him, but he caught a slight nod that said, "Yes." Good. She was ashamed of it, then. Always a positive sign.

"What did he do to get you back?"

She began to rock, just slightly, and he prodded her again. "What, Katie?"

Suddenly, she looked at him, eyes full of tears, and said, "He killed them. Like he's planning to kill you tomorrow."

Fargo reached across and grabbed her, through the old calico of her skirt, by one knee. "This a habit with him?"

No words, just a slow and deliberate nod. And then her tears began to fall, trailing down her high-planed cheeks. "Seven times," she volunteered softly. "You make the seventh one."

He let go of her leg and sat up straight. "I ever tell you that seven's my lucky number, Miss Kathleen Dugan?"

She stared at him as if he'd just picked up a hatful of bumblebees and willingly jammed it onto his head. "Are you crazy?"

Fargo laughed, and not softly. He sure was crazy, all right, crazy like the proverbial fox, even though at the moment he was laughing like a loon. He shook his head while he got his laughter under control long enough to ask, "What's the plan? Is he waitin' for us, down the trail to Tucson?"

She nodded a yes.

"Well, we just won't go that way. Make you feel better, Miss Katie?"

She let out a big breath, and allowed that it did. He believed her. At least, every bone and muscle of her body was speaking to him now, and they all said she was telling the truth. He trusted bone and muscle more than feminine wiles any day of the week. He stood up and calmly went back to his place, across the fire.

Her eyes followed him, this time with curiosity. "You don't wish to . . ." Her eyes dropped to the desert floor again. "You don't wish to use me?"

Which answered Fargo's unspoken question. Softly, he replied, "No, Katie, not unless you wish it, too.

Now, why don't we both try to get a little shut-eye so we can set out before the old rooster knows we're awake, all right?"

Her lips curved into a smile, even though she didn't look toward him, and she stretched out on the ground, using that ratty carpetbag for a pillow.

She was asleep in the time it took Fargo to roll himself a smoke. And snoring softly by the time he had it half smoked down.

Flicking his ashes to one side, he shook his head, chortling. Indian or white, good or bad, skinny or fat, when you took them down to the core, all women were the same.

"Mysteries," he muttered. He took a last, long drag on his smoke, then ground it out underfoot before he stretched out and pulled his hat down over his eyes. Tomorrow would bring whatever . . . well, whatever it had in mind.

Until then, he was going to rest in the arms of Morpheus.

He was asleep when the sun sank below the horizon.

"No, go that way."

The Trailsman grimaced and reined in the Ovaro. "What?" he barked. "There's nothing that way." Her hand pointed straight to the south, toward the Sand Hills.

"Go that way," she repeated, and gave her hand a shake, as if to underscore her words. "Over there. To the Sand Hills."

"Again, I'm askin' you why," he growled.

Against his back, she gave a sigh. "Because it is the only safe way. I wish to put as much distance between myself and Stubbins as you do, and I have better reason."

Fargo sat there a moment longer, his fingers softly drumming the saddle horn. She could be trying to talk him into riding into a trap, but he truly believed her story of having been sold and sold and sold again, only to be reclaimed.

He didn't think she wanted that to go on. And in the end, he had to believe her.

He reined the Ovaro in the direction she was indicating and pushed him into a fast walk, then a slow jog.

She breathed a small "Thank you" into his back, then leaned against him, resting the side of her face between his shoulders. Some of his initial anger had drained away, but he still felt as jumpy as a frog on a stove lid.

We can do this, she was thinking as he turned south and started toward the Sand Hills. She would wait until the formation came into sight, and then guide him toward it. *We can get there, and in plenty of time. Thank you, God; thank you, Jesus; thank you to all the gods of my mother's people. Thank you for sending me such a pliant savior, one whose heart can be molded and whose desires can be changed. . . .*

As they rode, her head pressed to the Trailsman's back, her mouth silently formed the words "Thank you, thank you, thank you," over and over again.

3

At about three o'clock in the afternoon, when the Trailsman was trying to figure out where the hell they were going at the same time he scouted for someplace to stop for the night, Kathleen Dugan, whom he now thought of as "Silent Katie," sat up and began to point toward the east. He looked toward it before he glanced back at her, and saw nothing to indicate there might be either a town or a stopping place. He let his breath out in a long, slow sigh.

"What?" he asked. They hadn't spoken a syllable of conversation since he stopped for lunch, and all their discourse had consisted of, at that time, was a few sentences from him and a grunt and a nod from her. He'd given up. She just wasn't going to talk, and that was that.

He twisted back to look at her. "Why?" he added, although he expected no answer in return.

But she said, "A place to camp."

He was so stunned that he just sat there for a moment before giving an eastward nudge to the Ovaro. And how did she know where there was a place to camp, anyway? To the best of his knowledge, she hadn't been this way before, either.

He asked, "How do you know?" without expecting an answer.

But, just as quickly as if they'd been holding a normal discourse over the last two days, she replied, "I was there once before. The place has water, game, and shade, Fargo."

He didn't know which shocked him more—that she had used his name, or that she'd mentioned water, game, and shade. The first was surprisingly pleasant, but the last three were necessities they were desperately short of.

About an hour later, he was more than pleased to round a low hill and come upon an oasis in the desert: water, game, and shade, just as promised. Here the desert floor had been gouged out so that a short portion of some river, forced underground by the terrain, surfaced, if only for a few feet. He could tell that during other seasons the pond was much bigger, but he wasn't about to turn down a few feet of fresh water. Neither, he could tell, was the Ovaro, who tugged at the bit eagerly.

"All right, boy," he said softly, and the horse moved forward, down toward the green patch of Mexican palms and verdant scrub below.

Fargo felt movement behind him, then heard the girl sigh and whisper, "At last."

He didn't know about the "at last" part, but he was mighty glad to see the water and the trees. He rode straight down to the water, then let the girl slip down before he dismounted. The Ovaro got right to business and buried his muzzle in the water, practically inhaling it. Katie was right behind him, he noticed, flopping on her belly and drinking deep from the little pond. And he wasn't far behind them.

Later that afternoon, when they'd finished their supper of jackrabbit and biscuits made with quail eggs, he took the time to look around. At first, it was just as he'd seen when they rode down into the little oasis: sand hills and more sand hills. But now that he was taking his time, he saw just the edge of a craggier hill sticking out a little past the edge of the one on the far right.

He narrowed his eyes, taking a closer look, then stood up and walked a few feet toward it. Craggier, yes. Made of stone, most certainly. Out of place? Definitely.

But the Arizona Territory was a land full of surprises and things that didn't belong, so at last he simply shrugged his shoulders and went back to his place beside the little fire. If Katie had noticed it, she gave no sign. She was busy fiddling with her moccasins.

He sat down and picked up his coffee again. After a long drink, he thought he would try again to get some conversation started. If she didn't want to talk, well, she wouldn't, and he'd be out nothing.

If she did, on the other hand, well, he'd have somebody to talk to, at least.

He leaned one elbow back against the rock his back was toward, and studied her for a moment before he said, "So, you been around here all your life, or just most of it?"

Surprisingly, she answered him. "All of it," she said, although she didn't look at him. "My first years were spent very near here. In a mountain. My father was a miner."

He chocked his head. This was the longest she'd ever spoken to him, and he was in a slight state of shock. Finally he managed to ask, "You lived in a mountain? You mean, in one of your daddy's old digs?"

"Yes."

Curiouser and curiouser. If it had been close, he'd

bet money it was in that big hunk of rock he'd just sighted. He tried again.

"Your daddy after silver or gold, Katie?" he asked.

"Both. He found mostly silver, though." She turned to look at him. "Mama said it was silver, anyway."

He nodded. "Mothers are usually right," he allowed. And then he thought of something. "If that hill isn't too far off, would you like to go there? To visit it?"

She sat straight up, like a hearth-loving dog that's just been asked if it would like to go for a walk, and said, "Yes, yes, I would!"

"All right, then," he replied, pulling his blanket up as the last rays of the sun sank below the western horizon. "In the morning, then."

The next day—Monday, as he figured it—he found she was as talky as a pet myna bird. In fact, she wouldn't shut up! She talked about the desert and the hills and the rocky almost-mountain that they were headed toward. She rattled on about the folks in Tucson (whom she didn't like), about Stubbins (whom she *really* didn't like), and about her parents, whom she missed very much.

She told him that they had lived in an old tunnel, approachable from the north. Her father had blown several rooms into it so that it was much like a house, except cooler in the summer (which was music to Fargo's ears) and warmer in the winter. In fact, she made it sound like a little slice of paradise. The only reason her mother had left it, she said, was that she had exhausted the game and there was nothing to eat aside from what they grew in their truck patch. And her mother wasn't much of a shot with either a bow and arrow or a gun.

So they had gone north, eventually running into Mr.

Stubbins, who gave them shelter in exchange for her mother's labor in the fields and around the cabin, and later, Katie's. It hadn't been Katie's favorite arrangement, and after her mother's death, he had falsified her bond papers to boot.

In fact, most of what he had told Fargo was a lie, if Katie was to be trusted, and he figured that she was. And God, she was pretty! He figured that just one good look at her could knock a songbird from its perch.

After about three hours of nonstop female chatter—for which he was mighty glad—she pointed ahead, toward the rocky hill that had just come into sight. "There," she said, arm outstretched. "There was where our front door was."

He squinted, and just thought he could make out a dark space at ground level. He could also see the place her mother had most likely raised her truck patch. It was overgrown with dying weeds and a couple of jackrabbits nosed through the undergrowth, but there was part of a falling-down, rectangular rail fence left around it. Several young pumpkins trailed out through what was left of the western fence.

They rode around the garden—more out of respect than anything else—and up to the base of the hill, next to the gaping door. It wasn't rectangular, but he could see where someone had chipped at it, trying to make it so. He let the girl slide down, and he followed, looping his reins over what was left of a hitching rail to the right of the opening.

When he looked at Katie, she was standing with her hands over her mouth and tears streaming down her face. For the moment, he didn't disturb her. He simply stood and waited.

After a few minutes she seemed to have control of herself. Wiping her eyes quickly with the back of her hand, she stepped forward and through the doorway.

Fargo followed, although he had the presence of mind to strike a match first. It was darker than the inside of a black hog in there.

The doorway turned into a short tunnel, walled by solid rock, then opened up into a sort of vestibule where a table stood guard, its tablecloth rotted and its legs rat-chewed and strung with cobwebs. Off this opened three "rooms," and she took him into all three. The first was her parents' room, large enough, granite walled, and with a four-poster bed that had seen better days. Here, he also picked up a lantern that seemed to have a bit of fuel in it. It lit just fine and he proceeded to carry it.

Second was a little girl's room—Katie's room—filled with homemade toys and dolls and more rats and spiders than he could shake a stick at. There was a pair of rattlers in the corner, too, and he gave them wide berth. Katie was close to tears again, and he took her arm, saying, "Later, honey. Show me the rest, all right?"

They went through the third room, which turned out to be the largest of them all. There was a sort of parlor, whose upholstery was long since ruined by heat and burrowing animals. The few occasional tables and the desk seemed to be pretty much all right, though, as did the several oil lamps. Beyond that, past a slight narrowing of the room, was a kitchen.

An ancient woodstove sat against one wall, with a stove pipe running upward to what he could only assume had been a vent at one time, and the sink drained outward, through a channel cut into rock three feet thick. There were cupboards for food and dishes that no longer remained, and a crude table and chairs for eating. A baby's high chair sat in the far front corner, draped with dusty dish towels.

Fargo had to admire it. It had taken a lot of work

on the part of Katie's father to build the place. And as far as he could tell, it was practically Indian-proof. The only way in or out was that front door, and on his way in, he'd seen several heavy backup doors that could be hung with no trouble in the narrow passage.

"I want to go back to my room," Katie announced.

"Hang on a second. Lemme get rid of those rattlers I saw in there." He searched around and found an old mop, shook it out, then headed back toward her childhood bedroom, where he corralled the snakes. Then he threw them outside, toward the garden. He checked under and behind all the furniture, and inside the chifforobe and drawers, before he let her come in again. The snakes hadn't been very old, and he didn't want to take a chance of there being a nest of them anywhere in there.

"It's okay, Katie," he said, setting aside the mop and ushering her inside. "No more snakes."

She paused midstride. "Snakes will not harm me. My mother made a charm."

She said it with such surety that he almost believed her. It was obvious that she believed herself.

She crossed the small room to the bed and sat on the edge of it. Her eyes closed and her lips curved into a smile, and softly she began to hum. He recognized it, but couldn't put a name to it. It was a lullaby Apache mothers often sang to their wee ones.

She closed her eyes and looked to be there for the long haul, so he turned his attention to more pressing matters: the Ovaro and their dinner, for starters. He stepped outside, stripped the stallion of tack, and at the last minute decided to bed him down inside. The sun had to be as wearing on him as it was on Fargo, after all.

He finally bedded the horse down in the parents' old bedroom—after checking for snakes, of course— fed and watered him, and closed off the room with a spare door from the entry hall turned sideways. Next, he turned his attention to dinner.

The grub bag was nearly empty again, so he made a short trip outside, where he shot the two rabbits he'd seen dining in the truck patch and picked a few vegetables that had managed to survive. Tomatoes and onions he got, plus a couple dozen pea pods. He figured that the lost river—the one that surfaced in the little oasis a few miles back—must wind under here, too. Enough of it, anyway, to keep a few plants alive.

By the time Katie resurfaced, he was in the kitchen, busily roasting the rabbits and stewing tomatoes and boiling peas. The vent for the stove wasn't as clogged as he had first feared, and the kitchen sink pump worked fine, once he primed it with water from his canteen. It was a little rusty at first, but cleared after a couple dozen good cranks.

"Smells good," she said, offering him a small smile.

"Thanks," he replied. "Still using spices and such from my grub bag, but the rabbit and the vegetables are fresh. Such as they are, I mean." He popped a lid back on the tomatoes. "Made your folks' room into a temporary stall for my horse. Hope you don't mind."

Actually, it didn't matter if she did. The horse was there, and that was that.

But she shook her head. "Do as you wish. I just wanted to see my bedroom again."

"It's smaller than I remember."

" 'Course," he said with a grin. "Last time you were in it, you were a heap smaller, too. The room looked bigger to you back then."

She returned the grin, saying, "I suppose you're right. It's all perspective, isn't it?"

He found himself noticing, not for the first time, the soft bell of her hips. He'd bet money that the legs beneath that cheap, calico skirt were long and lean, too.

And while he was staring at her, he heard a noise. She heard it too, because she looked up quite suddenly at the sound. It *had* come from above—but how could solid rock make a sound like a pickax?

"Are there tunnels above here?" Fargo asked.

She shrugged. "I don't know."

He dropped his spoon on the table. "Vegetables come off the stove in five minutes, rabbit comes out in fifteen. I'm gonna go check out that sound."

As she curiously nodded, he slipped from the kitchen, the parlor, and to the outside.

4

As silently as he could, he began to skirt the mountain, stopping every few feet to take a careful look upward. After half an hour, he was wishing he'd waited for his share of their dinner before he set out, but he kept on walking and looking. Nothing, there was nothing, not anywhere.

Until, that is, he had walked for a good hour and a half to the south side of the rise. Here, the mountainside was a sheer cliff of granite and basalt that rose up about thirty feet before it settled in to a slower incline. He was just about to round a low-growing cottonwood when he heard the voices.

He froze, holding his breath. He couldn't make out much of what they were saying, but they were talking American, not Mexican, and they were definitely not miners. Miners would be gabbing about blast placements and fingers of silver they'd spotted, and speculation about the price of silver back in Tucson.

These boys were bothered by no such concerns. The little scraps of language he was able to make out were more like, "Need a bigger room up on level three, Charlie," and "Somebody better finish up those gun ports on two." He heard something else that gave him pause—mentions of Abraham Lincoln, most of which were not very kind, to say the least. Lincoln was referred to as a "monkey's butt" on more than one occasion, and it made Fargo mad. Not mad enough to make a mistake, though: he held his peace, then silently snuck back the way he'd come.

In the hour and a half it took him to get back to Katie and the Ovaro, he did a lot of thinking. He had decided that those boys were agents of the wrong side—that side being the South—and that they expected the war to reach this far west. And they'd be ready for it, with their own fort and arsenal ready, and virtually impregnable.

He wondered how long it would be before they got around to checking the base of the north side of the mountain. They hadn't been there yet: this was obvious by the lack of tracks, and the fact that nothing, inside or out, had been touched by human hands for many years before he and Katie came along.

He said nothing to her when he came in. She had the table set and the meal was ready to go, if a little on the cold side. Still, he enjoyed every bite and complimented her as if she'd cooked it from scratch herself. She ate silently but greedily, as if the two jackrabbits he'd roasted might get up and hop away, and take the vegetables with them. When they'd each had their fill, he produced a surprise for dessert: a small watermelon, picked from the corner of the garden.

She fairly squealed at the sight of it, and he laughed. "Hold on, there, princess. Gotta see if it's as good on the inside as it looks on the outside."

He pulled out his bowie knife and sliced it in two with one deft motion. Sure enough, the inside was a rich pink dotted with black seeds, and he smiled. He cut one half of it into four slices, which he handed to her, then cut up the other half for himself. It was ambrosia, and she saved the seeds in a little glass jar she found in the cupboard.

He'd planned on telling her what he'd learned after they had dinner, but now he found himself with nothing to say. Would the presence of those men frighten her? Would it make her angry and set her off on the warpath? He had no way of knowing how she'd react or, for that matter, if she'd react at all. It was a puzzlement.

But she solved his dilemma for him. After they were comfortably settled in before the little woodstove, she asked him, "Were there men? When you walked around the mountain?"

He couldn't evade a question so direct, so he said, "Yes, there were."

"Digging?"

"Yes again, but not for silver. I think they were digging some kind of a hideout."

She lifted a brow curiously. "A hideout?"

He told her everything he'd heard then, and what he suspected the men were up to, and she listened attentively.

And then, much to his surprise, she said, "We must do something. I know of these men. Stubbins used to speak of them often. He was their friend. He was on their side. He said that when war came, the South would strangle the North, and he would be there to watch."

She paused, setting her mouth into a grim line before she spoke again. "We cannot allow this to happen," she said with finality, as if there would be no more discussion to the contrary. As if there had been any before.

Fargo nodded. "I agree. But it's not safe with you—"

"Safe enough," she cut in.

He mulled this over for a moment before he said, "All right. Any ideas?"

"Their leader is called Bates. He may be here, or he may not be. He goes to town often, to sell the silver ore they find in my father's claim."

Fargo waited for her to go on.

"This is not right!" she said with some vehemence. "It was my father's, and it should be mine now."

He asked, "You more upset about the war plot, or their stealing your silver?"

"Don't be an ass," she replied. "The war, of course. But the silver is important, too. It is mine."

He took her at her word, and said no more. That was, until about fifteen minutes later, when she spoke again.

"There is a secret way up to the second level in my room," she said. "My father was mining up there when he died. Mother said his heart just gave out. The way is narrow and steep, and comes out in a little nook that he blew out with dynamite. Or it did. I don't know what changes they have made."

"Do they know about your old living quarters?" Fargo asked.

She shook her head. "Not that I know of. Even Stubbins did not know. It was mother's and my secret. She always said that someday we would steal away from Stubbins and come back here to live. We tried three times, but he always found us, beat us, and brought us back to his shack, each time with more work to do."

"Sorry," he said. He really meant it.

She studied the floor at her knees. Without looking up, she asked, "You do not wish to use me?"

This was an answer he had to phrase very carefully, and he knew it. Slowly, he said, "I wish to very much, but only if you want to. It ain't my way to take a woman by force."

She turned her head to look up at him, and her eyes were full of desire. And curiosity.

She reached for him first, which surprised him. But

28

he let her feel the texture of his beard, then run her fingers through his hair over and over, let her feel the curve of his brow and the hard curve of his jaw before he touched her face, too. It was soft, soft as if the wind had not touched it in all her years. She was blushing a little now, and he kissed the tip of her nose, just a brush of a kiss, before his hand went to her temple.

"My Katie," he whispered. "How beautiful you are."

Her blush deepened as if she'd never been told this before, and he was shocked. How could no one tell this girl how beautiful she was? He sat up to pull off his buckskin shirt, and was surprised when his sunburn didn't hurt. Next came the boots and the britches, and when he looked at her again, she was nearly out of her calico skirt and blouse.

She was stunning. Her blue eyes were heavily fringed with dark lashes, her mouth upturned, her neck like a slender pillar connecting to shoulders both delicate and shapely. Her breasts were much larger than he had imagined, full and round and crowned with salmon nipples that were already puckered. Her waist was narrow, and belled gently into full, muscular hips and lean thighs. He would have taken a fuller roster, but just then she kissed him, her mouth pressed to his.

The kiss was firmer than he had expected, and he resolved to teach her how to kiss. "Easy, baby," he whispered, once she gave him a chance. "We've got all night."

She nodded, and this time he went in for the kiss, holding her naked body pressed to his, teasing her mouth open, and letting his tongue make gentle incursions into hers.

She was a quick study. Soon they were kissing deeply, while Fargo's hands explored her body and she explored his.

He let his head drop to her bosom, found a nipple and ringed it twice with his tongue before taking it into his mouth. This was something she had never experienced before, because she gave a sudden gasp, then gripped the back of his head, urging him on while she whispered, "Yes, yes . . ."

While he suckled her breast, one hand traveled slowly down her belly toward the dark triangle at the juncture of her legs. When it found its target, even though he only touched it gently, she spasmed. He took advantage of the situation by raising his lips to hers once again, and easing her legs apart. Deftly, he moved between them.

He did not enter her yet, though. He kept on tickling, teasing, stroking her until he felt the bud inside grow large and hard beneath his fingers, and only then did he begin to ease himself where he wanted to be.

Slowly, slowly he went, and she gasped with his every move, until his shaft was buried up to the hilt. He could feel her interior muscles pulling, pushing at him, and decided he'd waited long enough. In fact, he didn't know that he could wait any longer.

With a mighty rush, he withdrew nearly all the way. Then he pushed back inside, repeating the motion over and over again. He felt her spasming beneath him even as he was caught in the throes, too, and three strokes later, they were finished.

He didn't pull out right away, though. He enjoyed the aftershocks, simple spasms of muscles, that a lady had once she was fully satisfied. And satisfied this one was. It occurred to him that she had never had an orgasm before. After all, as far as he knew, her only experiences had been rapes. This thought made him angry, but she didn't notice. She was busy grinning like a sated fool with her eyes closed and her long, lean legs still wrapped around him.

5

The next morning, the boys upstairs were quiet, and Fargo passed the time by seeing to the Ovaro while he gave thought to what their next move should be. "This would be a lot easier if I had a troop of cavalry in my hip pocket," he mumbled more than once. It was true that they certainly lacked in numbers, but it was also true that they had surprise on their side. For all the good that would do them. He thought about sending up smoke signals, but that would bring Apache a whole lot faster than it would the cavalry, who were about a hundred miles away.

He didn't know which would be worse: to be taken by Apache or the men digging above them. Certainly the latter would be far worse for Katie than it would for him, but the former wouldn't be any bed of roses, either. And then, the men doing the digging were bound to spot the smoke signals before anybody else. He was at a loss.

Katie, however, didn't seem to have a care in the world. She hummed as she tidied the living room and kitchen, washing dishes and throwing out things that had been ruined by time and exposure. By the time he finished feeding, watering, grooming, and rebedding the Ovaro, the kitchen sparkled like it had never suffered any disuse at all.

"You like?" she chirped.

"Very much," he said. "You've got the place lookin' brand spankin' new!"

She smiled at him and said, "Thank you, Mr. Fargo."

He gave a small bow. "You're welcome, Miss Dugan."

She laughed, and suddenly he thought of a question. "Those Apache your mama left behind. You think they'd take kindly to seein' you?"

She pursed her lips. "I don't see why not. She was a princess, you know."

He slid into a kitchen chair. "A princess?"

"She was the daughter of . . . Bloody Spear, I think you would call him. He was the war chief of the Chiricahua Apache. Mother's band, at any rate."

Now, Fargo had had himself some dealings with Apache, both good and damned bad, and he wasn't about to take a chance on having his brain roasted while he was still alive, or having the skin peeled off his living body. He still had a scar on his back from where they had started, once upon a time. He would never forget the pain. He would also never forget Lance Bryan, his old friend from the army, who had saved him. God bless old Lance. . . .

He said, "How far off is this Bloody Spear camped this time of year? Close enough to see smoke signals?"

She pondered this for a moment, then said, "It is hard to tell with him. According to my mother, he could be anywhere from deep in Mexico to nestled into the Santa Rita mountains." She shrugged her shoulders.

"Hm," he grunted. It didn't look like they were going to get any help from the Indians, and help from the whites was too far away to even think about. He'd have to go back to square one.

"My uncle, Howls at the Moon, would be camped nearer, though," she added. "He stays to the south in the Sand Hills, close to the Mexican border. He says that Mexican flesh smells sweeter than American when it burns."

A chill, unbidden, ran up Fargo's spine. He'd heard tell of Howls at the Moon. He liked to ambush Mex freighters and wagon trains, tie the survivors to the spokes of the wheels, then set them ablaze. He didn't much want to meet Howls at the Moon—in this life or the next one. Or the one after that either, if there even was such a thing.

"Any other relatives camped close by?" he asked, not really wanting to hear the answer.

But she said, "Not unless you wish to count Cuchillo Rojo—that is, Red Knife. He is not blood kin, but I know that he took a white wife a few years back. She is called Glows Like Sun."

This gave Fargo a little more to chew on. He asked her, "How far away is he camped, do you think?"

Again, she shrugged. "Could be to the north, could be to the south. Mother said he moved camp often to keep the army at bay."

Fargo thought over his possibilities. Howls at the Moon was out—he had no wish to be tied to a wagon wheel and roasted like a Christmas goose. And between Bloody Spear and Red Knife, he figured a man with a white wife might be a tad more understanding about Katie. And himself.

"Can you send smoke signals?" he asked.

She looked at him as if he'd suddenly grown two heads. "Of course I can. My mother taught me."

He nodded. "Then tomorrow, if I take you to a far-off mountaintop, can you send a smoke signal to Red Knife? Ask him to help us?"

She didn't answer right away, just looked at her

33

hands, her jaw working side to side. "Perhaps," she said at last. "But I can tell him nothing about Mr. Lincoln or the war. He will have no truck with such."

"But will he come and save us from those men up in the mountain?"

"Yes," she said, nodding. "That I believe he will do."

"And he won't harm us in any way?"

She shook her head. "That would be bad medicine. If you will take me someplace safe, I will send the message."

Fargo grinned. "Deal," he said.

She smiled back at him.

After a night of passionate lovemaking, the pair set out at dawn the next morning. Fargo was careful to travel the passages where he was reasonably certain they could not be seen, even on the slim chance that one of the men had managed to scale the mountain. By the time they stopped for lunch, they were more than halfway to the peak he'd picked out, and by mid-afternoon they were there. It wasn't a high precipice, just high enough that their smoke would rise straight and clear, and be visible for miles in every direction. The day was windless, and he counted that as a sign that God was on their side. He wasn't much of a praying man, but he let loose with a silent prayer.

They needed all the help they could get, and he wasn't too proud to ask for it.

He built a fire, fueled with mostly green wood because he wanted a lot of smoke, and when it was blazing and smoking away, he handed Katie the Ovaro's saddle blanket. "Go to it, girl," he said.

Grimly, she took the blanket from him, crouched beside the fire, and began signaling.

By dusk, he had seen no sign from either the outlying areas where Cuchillo Rojo might be, or the mountain men slicing into Katie's home. They were up high enough that he could have seen the miners, had they been followed, through any number of passes through the hills, so he breathed a sigh of relief. "Put out the fire, baby," he told Katie.

She looked up. "I can still signal for a good half hour, yet," she said, a question in her eyes.

Fargo shook his head. "If Cuchillo Rojo was there to see them, he would have answered. So would anybody else, I reckon. I'm afraid we're gonna have to give up and go back."

Grudgingly, she kicked dirt and sand over the fire until it was out, then handed him back the Ovaro's saddle blanket. It stank of smoke, but he didn't think the Ovaro would mind. Frankly, he didn't care. All he could think about was another way to find help, and he was coming up empty at every turn.

It looked like he and Katie were going to have to turn tail and run for Tucson, and hope somebody there was on their side. Arizona, after all, planned to be on the side of the Confederacy, for all the sense that made.

Well, he'd break it to her tomorrow. She'd had enough rough work for today. After he tacked up the Ovaro, he climbed on and helped her up behind him. Then they set off down the mountainside: he appeared dejected and she was grinning, her arms looped about his waist and her head pressed happily to his back.

Katie Elizabeth Dugan, whether she knew it or not, had been born a very lucky child. Lucky to have a mother who had loved her more than anything, lucky to have a drunkard of a father who had owned the good sense to die when she was very young, and lucky to have been picked up by Stubbins, who, in turn, had brought her to Fargo.

Now, Stubbins had sold her to a number of the

wrong sorts of fellows along the way, but it had to be argued that eventually, he'd gotten her to Fargo. And just, as fate would have it, in the nick of time.

As they rode back toward her old home in the hillside, Katie hugged his back and thanked her lucky stars—and surprisingly, Stubbins—for putting the two of them together. She knew she was a lucky girl, despite everything, and she was grateful.

She saw no one, and no sign of anyone besides themselves having passed, indicating to her that they hadn't been followed. She knew Fargo was looking, too, and that she probably shouldn't bother, but four eyes were better than two to her way of thinking.

Suddenly, Fargo reined in the Ovaro. She looked up to find him staring out to the left, and she followed suit. At first she couldn't see a thing out of the ordinary—low scrub, unblemished; weedy saplings; the occasional prickly pear or jumping cholla; a lone black-bird and a covey of California quail—but after staring a moment, she saw what he was looking at: a lone hoof-print, unshod.

Looking closely, she also saw the drag marks where someone had tied a chunk of brush to his horse's tail and pulled it behind him to hide his passage. The hoofprint that still showed was near a jumping cholla, where the horse had stepped wide around it. Having had experience with the cactus, she was not surprised by the horse's actions.

This horse had been leaving their home, not going toward it, so she wasn't concerned about being bush-whacked in her own room. And since it was not shod, she doubted it belonged to the white men digging out her father's silver. Instead, it was likely an Indian pony. Someone must have seen her smoke signals, after all. Someone close.

She prayed silently that it was so, that someone would come to help her reclaim her birthright.

Ahead of her, Fargo suddenly clucked to the horse and they began to move again. Apparently he had come to the same conclusion that she had about being bushwhacked, for he showed no fear, and she felt none in his sturdy spine nor his core.

She turned her head again to watch for signs on the right and once more nestled her head into the wide, shallow dip between his shoulder blades. She was learning more and more about a man's body through him, and about her own. She had never known that lovemaking could be so sweet, so caring. In fact, she had never heard it called "lovemaking" before, only "doing the dirty" or "using" her.

Fargo was the best, the best in the world. And she knew that her father had been just as nice with her mother.

Another hour, and they would be home. She smiled.

Fargo was busy making plans, or trying to. He had seen no answering smoke signals, so he had to figure that Cuchillo Rojo was too far off to have seen them. But the track he'd seen in the desert, the single track not obscured by the brush drag, both gave him hope and set his spine turning to aspic.

If it had been a member of a halfway friendly tribe—one that would be friendly to Katie and her man, that was—then he figured to be sitting in clover.

But if the passing brave had been one of Howls at the Moon's men, well, he figured his goose was pretty well cooked. Not to mention the rest of his body parts.

So far as he could tell, the brave—if it had been a brave at all, and not just a passing Mexican too poor to shoe his horse—had been alone. Perhaps he was a scout sent out to see just who was sending those signals. They could have ridden right past him almost anywhere. Apache were known to melt into their surroundings. But if this was true, and they hadn't received a couple of arrows in the back, it boded well. Didn't it? He tried to tell himself so, at any rate.

He was afraid they had to make do with the single partridge he'd shot while they were up on the mountain and she was sending smoke signals. He'd cleaned it on the spot, plucked it, too. He didn't want to fire off his gun so close to the miners. Or Rebs. Or whatever they were.

Their rocky shelter came into view, and he whoaed the Ovaro and gave the place a good looking-over before he was ready to move ahead again. Everything seemed as they had left it. No tracks disturbed the garden.

Still, he said to Katie, "Be quiet until I tell you different. I want to make sure we don't have any unwelcome company."

He felt her nod, "Yes," against his back, and urged the Ovaro forward.

6

No one had been in their cave. That was, outside of a young jackrabbit, which Fargo chased outside. While he saw to putting the Ovaro up for the night, Katie made dinner, and ended up surprising him by making so much out of so little.

They had a fine partridge stew and deviled eggs, which she had found up by the signal fire and hadn't told him about. There was a kind of flat bread for which she had ground the flour, yesterday, between two flat rocks, and a sort of pudding made from pumpkin and some sort of sweet root she had found growing wild in the garden. All in all, it was a tasty, filling meal, and Fargo told her so.

She blushed and grinned. "Thank you," she said. "Was there enough?"

"Just right," he replied, and held his hand up to her. When she took it, he grinned and pulled her down onto his lap.

She took this as an invitation to instigate sex, but after a lingering kiss, he pulled away from her. "A little later, Katie," he said. "First we have to do some strategizing."

She cocked her head. "Some what?"

"Figure out what we're gonna do next. If the Apache don't come, I mean."

"But—"

His finger went over her lips, quieting her. He said, "I know you must've seen that Indian pony track back in the pass, yes?"

She nodded.

"Well, that don't mean somebody's coming. He didn't step out along the way to say so, did he? He might have been a brave out all on his own, or a Mex trader or something. We can't count on seeing that one track to mean anything."

"But—"

Again he quieted her. "I think the best thing, all in all, is for you and me to cut over to Tucson first thing in the morning. I know a few fellows who'll—"

This time, it was her finger that covered his lips. She shook her head. "No, Mr. Skye Fargo, Mr. Infamous Trailsman. They will come. I know it."

He had to admit that his spirits lifted momentarily, but he asked, "And how do you know this? Did you see some far-off smoke signals that I missed?"

She giggled and shook her head. "No, Fargo, but they will come, Cuchillo Rojo and his people. I know this as sure as I know I am alive and sitting on your lap this very minute."

She seemed convinced right down to her moccasins, but he wasn't so sure. "But you can't give me anything concrete, can you?"

She lowered her head in a most confidential way, then whispered in his ear, "I could tell you, my Fargo, but then I would have to kill you." And then she pulled her head back up, looked directly into his eyes, and smiled widely.

He shook his head, but he was grinning. "You're that sure?"

"The first thing in the morning, they will come. Well, maybe the middle of the morning."

She was convinced, pure and simple. But he still

couldn't take the chance. "All right," he said, and he felt her relax. "But if they haven't come by midmorning—"

"Then we're off to Tucson," she said, finishing his sentence for him.

"Very good," he said, wrapping both arms around her and hugging her. "Now, what do you think we should do in the meantime, Miss Katie Dugan?"

"Oh, Fargo!" she said with a little squeal, and planted an eager kiss on his waiting lips.

Morning came too soon for Fargo. He was up with the dawn, and took up his station on a chair in the barricaded front hall, his rifle across his lap.

By eight o'clock, there was no sign of anyone coming, let alone a band of pissed-off Apache warriors out to rescue one of their women from a band of secretive—and thieving—white interlopers. Fargo went outside long enough to relieve himself and pull off an armload of fresh grass for the Ovaro, then returned to his post.

By nine, there was still no sign of Apache, although he could hear someone banging around too close above him for comfort. At nine thirty, Katie tiptoed up from the rear of the cave, tapped him on the shoulder, then looked up toward the sounds. Worry tugged at her features. He grabbed her hand and gave it a comforting squeeze. He didn't know how she felt about it, but he was ready to cut out for Tucson right now, before one of their uninvited neighbors fell right through their ceiling.

He was little more than halfway out of his chair when he spotted something outside that sat him right back down. With a jangle of harness and a rhythmic thud of hoofbeats, Stubbins, drawn by his old mule, came rattling toward them.

Fargo knew he was far enough back in the long,

shadowy hallway that he couldn't be seen from outside, but he hissed, "Down!" at Katie, and she hit the floor immediately, squatting beside his chair. She was shaking. He thought that Stubbins must bring it out in people, although he figured Katie's reasons were different from his.

He was close to the shakes himself, mainly because he was afraid he'd suddenly lose all control, march outside, punch Stubbins square in his lousy ax-blade face, and alert the boys above to their presence.

But Stubbins paid them no mind. In fact, he didn't give a second glance to the rock face that sheltered them. Instead, he whipped his mule into a trot and turned left, starting the long trip round the base of the mountain, presumably en route to see his friends.

"Didn't your mother ever tell him about this place?" he whispered.

Katie shook her head. "No, never," she whispered back. "It was our family's secret, and we held it dear, my mother and I." She furrowed her brow and added, "When you have little else, secrets are precious."

Fargo stroked her hair, then pulled them both to their feet. Overhead, someone was still chipping away. He wondered if they could be trying to make a scout whole up there. If they had any brains, they couldn't figure to tunnel straight down. After all, they didn't know that Katie's home was beneath their feet. All they could know was that it was just more solid rock.

Suddenly, he moved back toward the room that housed the Ovaro, dragging Katie along behind him. He hurriedly began to tack up the stallion while he whispered, "Get the grub bag from the kitchen. And any grub that's portable."

She understood, because she rushed from the room without uttering a syllable, and was back, toting a full grub sack, before he had the Ovaro's bridle halfway on his head. "Keep going," she whispered as she passed him and tied the grub bag up behind the saddle.

The getting around the mountain base was tough and rugged, but that didn't stop Stubbins. He was the first to tell anyone who asked that the dictionary showed his picture next to the word *tough* and that its definition was *rugged*. He'd be wrong, but that wouldn't stop him from saying it.

Over and over and over again.

He whipped the mule again, pushing him forward through the brushy, brittle undergrowth. He'd been here twice before—both times to see O'Rourke—and he had yet to figure out why there was such a difference in the desert growth from place to place. He'd ride through a wide patch of verdant green, wildflowers blooming and insects buzzing, and then twenty feet to the side it would be desert again and stay that way for a good long time.

He hadn't come to the underground river idea yet, but he'd settled fairly happily on the theory that the terrain underground was solid rock, close to the surface. And he was partially right.

At the moment, he was trying to clear a particularly stony portion of the track, if anyone but he would call it that. He came to a steep portion, whipped the mule again, but this time the mule—who was partially forgiving and easygoing, considering his species—would go no farther. He stopped in his tracks, and when Stubbins whipped him again, he simply sat down in his traces.

"Goldurn mule!" Stubbins shouted, and jumped down from the driver's bench. He walked forward, took the bridle in his hands, and shook it in an attempt to shake some sense into the mule's head.

Neither goal was met.

Stubbins let loose of the harness, stomped around

in a little circle, then faced the mule again. "All right, consarn you! You just stay here and rot for all I care, you good-for-nothin', dad-blamed, dumb beast!"

Stubbins walked off and left the mule and the rig where they sat. It wasn't much farther to the tunnel, and he'd make it faster on foot than trying to whip some sense into the mule.

The mule waited until Stubbins stumbled through the brush and out of sight before it slowly stood up with a low groan, then ambled off, pulling the wagon over to the right so that it was in the thin shade of the mountainside. Contentedly, he began to graze down a little patch of green.

Down below, Fargo was ready to strike out. He had already carefully checked outside to make sure that Stubbins was out of sight. He then went back in to retrieve Katie and the Ovaro. But he had no more than led the stallion outside, with Katie following timidly, when a great cloud of dust appeared on the northern horizon—or at least, what passed for a horizon from this vantage point: the opening of the little valley with its garden to the pass above.

"Get back in!" Fargo hissed, but when he turned around, Katie was standing stock-still and grinning ear to ear. "Katie!" he said more loudly. "Get inside!"

But she didn't budge. She only pointed toward the northern entrance to their valley.

He whipped back around to face it, and found himself staring into the faces of at least thirty Indians, who had managed to charge the rest of the way into the valley while he was trying to prod Katie into action. His gun would do him no good in the face of these odds, even if he could draw it immediately.

"Shit," he muttered under his breath while the Indians sat there. Waiting. Waiting on what was the question now.

Suddenly, he sensed motion at his side, and then heard Katie speak up. She spoke in what he thought was fluent Apache, although he didn't speak it himself. Just enough to parlay for trinkets and the like. But he did catch a few words that made sense to him.

"Cuchillo Rojo," for one. The leader of these men must be the great Red Knife, the one who had a white wife. That let Fargo relax a bit. He made out the word that meant "war chief" and another that meant "evening," and twice he made out his name being spoken, but he was pretty much at a loss for the rest of it.

Then the head warrior, the one he thought must be Cuchillo Rojo, spoke.

"Fargo," he said in a surprisingly clean accent. "I am come to help you and Daughter of Dancing Bird. She tells me you are a famous warrior amongst your people. My people know you as well."

"Not all that famous," Fargo said. Katie must have been bragging on him, although he couldn't figure out why.

Cuchillo Rojo shook his head. "She said you would say that." And then he broke into a long rant in Apache, aimed at Katie.

At last Katie nodded, spoke in Apache to him at length, then bowed her head and backed up. The Apaches backed their ponies, too, and then took off around the mountain on Stubbins' heels, traveling a great deal more slowly and cautiously than they had ridden in.

Fargo waited until the last pony was out of sight before he turned to Katie. He thumbed back his hat. "Now, how on earth did you know it was gonna be him?"

She smiled and took the Ovaro's reins from him before she pointed to her head. "Katie smart girl, like her mother," she said in pidgin.

He growled at her playfully. "I ought to . . ."

Calmly, she led the Ovaro back inside the doorway and back into blackness. Fargo scratched his head, then followed them inside.

He supposed all they could do now was wait.

7

"No!" Fargo repeated for roughly the fifth time.

This time, Katie sat up and slid her hand from his chest, a look of sorrow on her face. "Why? Am I doing something wrong?"

He sat up as well and gave his head a shake, telling himself, *The next time somebody offers to sell you a girl, run the other way!* He said, "We shouldn't be doing this—or even thinking about it—right now. I should be up there, fighting arm in arm with Cuchillo Rojo!"

Katie had the most gorgeous pout, which she chose that moment to use most effectively.

She said, "But why, Fargo? Cuchillo Rojo has come. His men have likely overpowered those thieving skunks already. They do not need you." She squirmed closer and put her hand back on his chest. "Me, on the other hand?" Gently, she splayed her fingers. "I need you. Oh, I need you very much."

He pushed her away, more roughly this time. "I said to cut it out." This time, he stood up and looked down at her. "I'm going out and up. I can't stand this waiting around."

He felt her hand grab his leg, and he stopped before he'd taken a step. "What?"

She tilted her head. "Take the shortcut, then. Through the wall."

When he furrowed his brow, she rose to her feet, too, and led him from the parlor back to her bedroom, and to the back wall. He didn't remember seeing any access hidden back here, but he held his peace. A good thing, too, because a moment later she knelt and lifted the edge of an old and dusty screen. She ran her fingertips along the narrow crack in the wall until a pressure plate, cleverly hidden—and constructed, too, he thought—gave way, and the door slowly swung out from the wall, stalling twice on the floor rubble.

But it opened while she said, "This was how my father would go up to mine," and Fargo could see that it was a very narrow passage, just wide enough for the steps that spiraled upward. He didn't know what he had expected—a ramp or a runway, or something—but it wasn't this. He stuck his head into the passage and peered up.

Nothing. Absolute quiet. Absolute darkness.

He dug into his pocket, pulled out a sulphur tip, and struck it to life on the granite passage wall. He held one finger to his lips, hissed, "Shh," then stepped inside. She pushed the door closed after him.

Alone in the dark on that eerie staircase, he began to make his way upward.

Long after he figured to have climbed enough steps to take him to the top of the Rockies, he finally dead-ended at a door. He was on his fourth match by then, and just had time to see where the catch was before the match burnt his fingers. He stood there in the darkness, ear pressed to the door, and heard . . . nothing. Quietly, he drew his sidearm, then released the door's catch.

The door swung quietly outward, but there was no bloodshed to be found, no wailing wounded, just more pitch black. Muttering, "Son of a bitch . . ." he struck a fresh match and found himself in, of all places, what looked to be an old storage closet.

Scattered about on the floor were elderly blasting supplies. Hooks in the walls held pickaxes, shovels, pails, and gloves, as well as what he assumed had been Katie's father's spare overcoat.

A little more searching, and he found the door. This one was wooden, but Fargo couldn't hear a blasted thing through it. Neither could he see any light through the cracks that crazed it. Maybe the fight had moved outside, or up to the top floor. He had no idea what kind of layout this place had.

Quietly, he lifted the door's latch, then slowly opened the door out into what turned out to be the tail end of an old shaft. By the spiderwebs he kept running into—and the rats, which ran from his path, squealing and squeaking—it looked to have been long abandoned.

Still, he halted and waited for the rodent population to calm down before he moved forward again, silently swatting spiders and skirting rattlesnakes as he went.

Downstairs, Katie waited fretfully, walking from the bedroom to the parlor and back again, over and over, occasionally peering in at the Ovaro, who still waited, fully tacked and ready to go. She tossed the possibility of simply mounting him and just taking off in her mind a few times, but soon gave it up. The mine was too important to her to simply abandon it.

And that was her primary reason for being here, and for staying. The mine. It was her only legacy, and she would, by God, have it. She imagined that she could work it herself—not as fast as a man could, but fast enough that when it was spring, two years from now, she would have enough money to go anywhere and do anything she wanted.

She wanted to go to Europe, where she wouldn't

be taken for an Indian half-breed. There, she imagined, people would be different and wouldn't look down their noses at her. She could marry into more money there and see the Continent and be happy. And if that husband should happen to die, then she would have his money, too, and move on again.

She had the rest of her life figured out. All it would take to get it started was this mine, and she had started that already. Damn those men overhead, anyway! If they hadn't been here, thieving their way into her family fortune, she could have sent Fargo on his way days ago, and already been digging out bright metal.

She ground her teeth just thinking about it, but then moved on again. Fargo had his uses. He was certainly brave. He'd taken her up to send smoke signals, he'd discovered the men currently being taken care of by the great Cuchillo Rojo, and there could be no man better at lovemaking than he. She was certain of this, so certain that she had even seriously considered giving up her plans for the rest of her life and just being Fargo's woman for as long as he wanted her.

But then reality set back in, and she steeled herself. *No more thoughts like that,* she told herself. *Your mother gave up her dreams for your father, and what did it get her? A lifetime of servitude with the pig Stubbins, an early death, and years of sorrow.*

She made a face and muttered, "Feh!" Her future would be brighter than her mother's. It would be brighter, in fact, than anything her mother had ever dreamt of.

Of this, she was certain.

Fargo continued to make his way forward in the shaft. It was brighter now, so that he could creep forward without a sulphur tip to guide his way, but he still heard no sounds at all, let alone sounds of battle.

This struck him as rather odd. By his figuring, he

should be close to the southern mouth of the tunnel, and therefore close to the battlefront. Still, no signs of any tribulation whatsoever could be heard.

Had the Apache not yet reached the entrance to the cave? Had all the miners suddenly gone off to town? Or were they more heavily fortified than he had imagined?

Perplexed, Fargo continued to slowly move forward.

Cuchillo Rojo had long since split his braves into differing scouting units, and now, as he stood out of sight, at the opening to the mine, he congratulated himself. He could move in first, surprising the whites as they ate their noontime meal. Then the braves farther to the south and hidden in the brush could cut off an escape to the neighboring hills.

And, of course, Slouching Wolf and his men, already around the south side of the mountain, hidden in deep brush, and perched overhead, above the entrance to the old silver mine, could drop down and cut off anyone trying to flee back inside the tunnel.

It was a good plan.

It was not the sort of tale that one could tell around the campfires of the war councils, but it was good enough that it could be shared casually around the camp, and with his wife, Glows Like Sun. And she, in turn, would share it with Sees Silver, when the boy was old enough to understand. This gave Cuchillo Rojo the most pleasure of all, knowing that his son would have yet another story of his father's cunning and skill to hear and be entertained by.

They had come across a wagon with a mule hitched to it back around the side of the mountain. Some of his men wanted to kill it now for a feast later, but he hadn't allowed it. The mules would still be there later. He did not plan the feasts. He only planned the battles that led to them.

A lone partridge called from the south, answered by another, just above the entrance to the tunnel. His men, signaling. In return, Cuchillo Rojo whistled back an answering call. Everything was set. His men were ready.

He signaled his men with a tick of his finger, and the attack began.

Coming along the tunnel, Fargo jumped when the Apache war whoops began. He steadied himself against the rocky wall, pulled back a black widow from his cuff, and quickly stomped it underfoot before he began to move forward once more, this time with considerably more haste.

He rounded the last bend, and now they were in sight. One man broke off from the struggling knot out at the campfire and headed toward the tunnel—and Fargo—at a run. Fargo barely had his pistol free of its holster when a brave dropped down from over the entrance, his knife in his teeth, and cut the white man down with one deft stab of the flashing blade.

Fargo backed up a few feet and quickly considered his options. He could go racing out there and be picked off—accidentally, of course—by one of the braves up above. He could take up a position inside the entrance and start firing, but things were moving so fast and furious outside that he was likely to hit as many Apache as he missed.

Or he could put his sidearm away and go quietly back the way he'd come.

The last possibility won out.

He holstered his pistol and began going back the way he'd come, thumbing a match from his pocket. Not that he needed it yet, but a man could never be too ready. He was about to light it in the growing gloom when he suddenly heard scuffling footsteps behind him and turned just in time to be bowled over by Stubbins.

"Hey! Hold it!" he called to the man's retreating form, but within seconds Stubbins was out of sight and the sounds of his footsteps had receded into nothing.

"God dammit," Fargo swore under his breath. Stubbins had been wounded—at least, there was a good bit of blood on his shirt—but not enough, apparently, to slow him down. As he stiffly stood up from the rocky floor, he wondered just how well Stubbins knew this place. Well enough to know about the staircase in the supply closet? He hoped not.

The sight of Franklin Q. Stubbins, his very own self, walking out of her wall ought to scare the living bejesus out of Katie. He knew it would surely curdle his own cream.

The Apache were doing fine on their own, he reminded himself. He had to get back to Katie's side before Stubbins did.

Flicking his match into light, he began to move back down the tunnel once more.

Stubbins hadn't gone far. Having reached the end of the tunnel and finding no way out, he had taken up a crouched position against the back wall. His gun was out, and he was ready for action.

He'd seen Frank Dilby fall out front, and Dewey Albertson, too, along with a few fellows whose names he never knew. Where the heck did all those blamed Indians come from, anyhow? He'd seen no sign of them on the way out. And no hostiles roaming the countryside had been reported in the newspaper that was still in his rig, back around the mountainside.

He'd be jiggered if he knew where they came from, but it appeared that they'd come, and they were on the warpath. It was bad enough that he'd lost his little half-Apache meal ticket, but this was the end. And he'd be fried if they were going to get him!

He therefore planned on shooting off a good-sized chunk of anything—man, beast, or errant wind—that came down that tunnel.

Echoing footsteps approached from up the tunnel. He propped the pistol on his knee and steadied the barrel. Holding his breath, he cocked the gun, put his finger on the trigger, and waited.

8

Fargo held the lit match high so that he could see where the hell he was walking. The rats had mostly cleared out, but there were still snakes dozing alongside the walls or slowly slithering after the rats. The snakes were all very large and very fat, too. He figured that rats must be good for the waistline, although he wasn't tempted in the least to try it out.

By his figuring, he had one more turn to take before he hit the final tunnel that would lead him to the stairs that would take him down to Katie and the cavehouse. And if he didn't miss his guess—and if Stubbins hadn't known about the hidden closet and the stairs, which Fargo couldn't imagine that he did—then Stubbins was likely waiting for him, gun drawn, somewhere around the bend.

Now, Fargo didn't particularly want to be shot by anyone, but especially not by Stubbins. Just the thought of the odious little man was enough to turn his stomach.

So he quickly checked the floor to make sure he had a clear path, then shook out his match. Gun drawn, he inched toward the bend in the tunnel, then stopped just before he came to it.

"Stubbins!" he shouted. "Stubbins, you down there? It's Fargo!"

*   *   *

In the darkness, Stubbins scowled. Fargo? The same Fargo that now had his little piece of trade goods? How many Fargos could there be, anyhow, especially out here? Momentarily, he smiled. There might be a way out of this, after all. And he could always kill Fargo later, he reasoned.

He cleared his throat, then hollered back, "Right, Fargo, right you are! Mighty relieved to hear your voice! Come on back, son." He figured that "son" was always a good thing to add. Made things feel more like family, didn't it?

He heard Fargo take a few tentative steps, then stop again. "Are you wounded? I mean, was that your blood on your shirt?"

Stubbins smiled. "Mine it was, sonny. I'm in need of a bed and some doctoring, I'm afraid." Actually, he felt the wet shirt more strongly than the knife wound at the moment. He wondered briefly if he was going into shock, then shoved the idea away. He didn't have time for shock at the moment. He figured the damn Indians could be creeping along that passage, closing in on Fargo, even as they spoke. He'd seen Cuchillo Rojo out front, and knew his reputation.

"Sorry to be an imposition on you," he added for good measure when Fargo didn't answer right away.

"I'm coming in," Fargo called. "Hold your fire."

Stubbins didn't lower his gun, though, not even when he made out Fargo's shadowy form moving nearer, not even when he felt movement slithering along his leg. *Blood loss,* he told himself, and went back to debating if it'd be better to kill Fargo now or later. As much as he would rather do it now, he decided he'd best wait at least until he learned whether Fargo had a plan for getting them out of here with their hair intact.

The footsteps came nearer, and Stubbins eased his

gun hand, along with his pistol, down from his knee and holstered the pistol. He felt something odd brush against his hand, something smooth and dry and definitely alive, and was just wondering what it could be when he heard the quick rattling hiss, more like a burst of steam, and felt something bite down on his leg, then let go just as quickly.

He cried out at the surprise of it before he realized what had happened, and what that smooth, dry creature had been.

"Snake!" he cried, and tried to scramble to his feet just as Fargo reached him and pulled him up. They both staggered and hit the opposite wall, while Stubbins clawed at his right thigh and spat, "Consarned, goddamned, fanged spawn of Satan! Apple-pushin' vermin!"

Immediately, Fargo pushed Stubbins back down to the tunnel floor and struck a match. "Where?" he asked.

Stubbins pointed to his right thigh, about halfway up and to the outside. Quick as a flash, Fargo pulled out his Arkansas toothpick and sawed a hole in Stubbins' pant leg, then ripped the cloth the rest of the way open.

"What the hell're you doin'?" Stubbins spat.

"Shut up, unless you want to die right here," Fargo said as he located the fang marks. It didn't look good. There was already swelling at the site, and discoloration was beginning to spread bluish fingers away from the wound.

Fargo's brow furrowed. Most rattlers—better than fifty percent, he reckoned—didn't inject enough poison with one bite to kill a man. This one looked to have fanged Stubbins with enough to kill three.

It was spreading fast, and Fargo, who had planned to cut into the bite, then suck the poison out, knew there was nothing he could do to help. He might as well help Stubbins down the stairs and let him die in a bed.

He folded his Arkansas toothpick and stuck it back inside his pocket, then helped Stubbins to his feet again.

"What's wrong?" the old man demanded. "How come you didn't do anything except chop up my britches?"

"Take it easy," Fargo whispered. "Let's get you downstairs before we consider any rash actions."

"Rash?" Stubbins asked him, a little too loudly. "What's rash about savin' my life!"

Fargo hushed him again, then started toward the closet door. It was easier to open from the outside than it had been from the inside, and he had Stubbins through the door and weaving his way through the old supplies on the floor within seconds.

"What the hell is all this stuff?" Stubbins asked him. He was already beginning to sound weak and frail.

While he lit another match and began to search for the trigger to open the door, Fargo told him, "Leftovers."

Stubbins slowly nodded his head, which was currently pointed at a shovel on the opposite wall. "Oh. From when they was minin'. I get you."

Fargo found the catch and released the door, although he had to move Stubbins out of the way to let it swing free all the way. He said, "Follow me as close as you can, all right?" He knew there was no room for them to move side by side. "If you feel yourself starting to fall, grab my shoulder but don't push on me. Okay?"

Stubbins, who was beginning to realize his plight, nodded dumbly and stepped through the opening behind Fargo.

There was no way for Fargo to reach behind him and close the door, so he began to lead Stubbins, as calmly as he could, down to the bottom. He figured he could come back up and get the door after he had the old man safely in Katie's care.

Around and around they went, Stubbins falling three times and weakly clinging to Fargo's shoulders most of the way down. Once he nearly knocked them both for a loop, and Fargo caught himself on a small stone outcrop just in time.

By the time they reached the bottom, Stubbins' full weight was leaning heavily against Fargo's back, and it took Fargo a few minutes of fumbling with the door to get it open. Katie must have been out in the kitchen, because she came dashing in at the same time the door swung open.

"Help me," Fargo said as he felt Stubbins slipping to the ground.

Katie got to Stubbins before he could bang his knees on the stone floor, and helped Fargo get him to her childhood bed. When they laid him on the covers, his face was already beginning to look bluish, and his stricken leg had swollen to nearly half and again its normal size.

Apparently, Katie had seen snakebite before. She didn't ask what had happened, only, "It's not good, is it?"

Fargo only shook his head. He doubted Stubbins would last until nightfall. He said, "Katie, I've got to go back up and latch the top door. I'll be right back, okay?"

She nodded yes, and he was off.

Katie studied her former captor. How small he looked, how weak. She could kill him right this instant if she slipped that pillow over his face. She doubted that Fargo would suspect her. He'd just think that the poison had worked faster than he expected.

But just then, Stubbins parted his blue lips and

groaned weakly. Katie grinned. Better to let him die this way—slowly and painfully. Better for her mother's spirit. Better for Katie, herself, to let him die naturally, in all the pain the snake had meant for him.

She sat on the foot of the bed and studied him. "When were you bitten?" she asked, not expecting him to hear or to answer. "Just now, or has it been even half an hour yet?"

There was no reply.

She heard the soft, faraway sound as Fargo closed the door above, then the thud of boots coming down the stairs. She stood up and moved to the linen closet at the bed's foot, opened it, and pulled out an old blanket.

"This will do," she muttered as she made certain there were no vermin lurking in it.

"Still the same?" It was Fargo. He closed the stone doorway behind him.

Folding the blanket in her arms, she said, "Worse."

"That for him?" Fargo asked, nodding at the blanket.

"After I shake it out, outside," she said. The blanket was so old and dirty that she wouldn't have given it to a dog. Well, if it had been between a dog and Stubbins, the dog would have won out. But she would have shaken it out first.

She started for the doorway, then stopped and turned back. "And Cuchillo Rojo?" she asked. "How does he fare?"

Fargo nodded. "He and his men are winning."

"Good," she said, nodding curtly, and walked through the doorway, toward the front hall and the outside world.

Cuchillo Rojo was indeed doing very well. His men had by this time killed all the white miners, even the three that were hiding on the top floor. His first inclination had been to burn the place out, but one room looked like a war chamber—what whites would call an "office"—and he knew that there would probably be papers that Fargo would want to see. He therefore ordered his men not to set it ablaze. There would be plenty of time for that later on.

His men dragged the last of the bodies from the cave, and began to strip them of anything of value. Eventually, they'd be thrown on the pile of white corpses down south of the tunnel.

Only one of his men had been killed, and only one was wounded. The one who was killed, Takes Wing, had been a poor warrior to begin with, and had made a mistake by thinking the whites would all fight alike. He had been stabbed by a miner's knife blade before the miner had been separated from his arm and, not coincidentally, his life.

The hurt man was River Otter, who was sitting in the whites' camp, cursing himself. As well he might. River Otter was too seasoned a brave to have taken a bullet in his arm when he could have easily turned to the side and avoided it. But what was done was done, and now River Otter was steeling himself for a visit from Bent Pipe, the medicine man. Cuchillo Rojo gave him a last look and turned away, shrugging. When one was pierced by a white's bullet, one had to expect a visit from Bent Pipe, no matter how ineffective one believed he was.

One of his men waved at him and indicated that they had taken thirteen guns and much ammunition. He was glad for the guns, but happier for the ammunition. He had only three men who had mastered the knack of the white man's firestick, but even they managed to miss more than they hit. None of them had come with him on this trip, but he hoped they would find that these bullets fit their guns. Screeching Hawk, especially. He was down to four bullets, he had said, and four bullets were not enough to kill a white man.

He walked toward Bristling Sleeper, who asked him if he could send men to go get the mule for their feast. Cuchillo Rojo had already thought about this, and decided against it. The mule might belong to the Daughter of Dancing Bird, and he would preserve it until he was informed to the contrary.

He shook his head, then, in Apache, said, "Eat instead the meat and other food you found inside the tunnels, and celebrate with the whiskey you found there, too."

Bristling Sleeper's face lit up. They had found a cache of smoked venison inside, along with many cans of peaches, beans, and peas, not to mention a nearly full case of Spring Branch whiskey. Smiling his gratitude, he went on his way to tell the other men.

9

Katie returned shortly and covered Stubbins, who was now shivering when he wasn't beset by convulsions. Fargo was worried—mostly about Katie—but she seemed nonplussed. Apparently she was used to men dying around her, or at least, maybe she was glad to see Stubbins go. Either way, though, Fargo would have expected more show of emotion from her. Perhaps it was the Apache in her that made her so stoic. Perhaps she just hated him that much.

All in all, it didn't really matter, he supposed. Stubbins was going to die—sooner, he expected, rather than later—and that was that. He'd never seen anybody taken so fast.

Katie was just finishing tucking Stubbins' shaking body into the bed when Fargo asked her, "Do you know if he's ever been snakebit before?"

She nodded, tucked in the last corner, and said, "Two times that I know of. Once when I was very small, maybe seven or eight, and once a couple of years ago. He always claimed he had magic over the snakes."

Fargo didn't believe it for a second, and apparently, neither did Katie. She spoke his thoughts when she added, "I think his snake run-ins were with grandfather snakes. No venom. He would never admit it.

He said both snakes were the biggest and meanest he'd ever seen, and that they both gave him the full measure of their poison."

"Figures," said Fargo, and stood up. He didn't have much to do besides wait to hear from the Apache, but he'd do almost anything to avoid sitting here and watching Stubbins die. Forcing a smile, he asked, "You got any lunch, Katie?"

"I can," came the reply, and she set off for the kitchen. She was humming. He thought it bizarre.

At the same time in Tucson, Matthew Forebush, Franklin Q. Stubbins' partner in crime, was finishing lunch at the Bluebird Café, and toying with his pie. He figured to hear back from Stubbins tomorrow sometime, and get his report on how the men in the mountain were coming along. He had another week before he needed to have his crew put together and move them out there, but it was a slow process, finding men you could trust, men who could keep their mouths shut, who were fervent about the South, and who knew about rock-breaking to boot.

So far, he had three. He needed at least seven more.

"Want cheese on that after all?" said a waitress, suddenly appearing at his shoulder, and she spooked him a little. He shook his head, though, and she went away without another question.

Sighing, he finished his pie just to keep her from bothering him again. He then pushed the plate away and began to dig in his pocket. He found the dollar and fifteen cents with no problem, then found her another ten cents for a tip, spread it on the tabletop, and took his leave.

He stepped out on the boardwalk and lit his cheroot. He found a perch on a bench in front of the café and began to look over the town. There wasn't much to see. Dead animals, buzzing with flies, pocked the side streets, and gangs of children, most of them Mexican, ran through the flies to make a game of jumping the corpses of dead dogs, mules, and goats. At least somebody had finally dragged off the steer that had remained for almost ten days, half butchered and crawling with maggots, in the square.

Some things never changed.

He flicked the ash off his cheroot and glanced west, toward the Santa Ritas. Stubbins was over there right now, seeing to business. He'd be back tomorrow afternoon or evening, he'd said.

And he's gonna be thrilled that I've only got me the three men so far, Forebush thought. Stubbins, upset, wasn't his favorite customer. Actually, Stubbins wasn't his favorite customer in any mood, but that was beside the point. He had to dig up some more men, today if possible.

He'd already put up notices where he could, for all the good that had done him, and now he started scouting the crowd. You'd think that most fellows who came to Arizona were fair handy with a pickax, wouldn't you? Of course, that wasn't his major problem. His major problem was finding dyed-in-the-wool Southerners out west. 'Course, everybody out here had come from somewhere else, but even the Southerners weren't as Southern as they'd been back in Mississippi or Georgia or Tennessee.

He ground out his cheroot. Damn it anyway! Wasn't there another man with the South coursing through his veins to be found in all of Arizona?

"Pardon me, suh," drawled a distinctly Southern voice on his right. He looked up to find a finely attired gentleman standing beside him—obviously just off the stage, since he carried a carpetbag and was mopping his brow with an enormous, oversized handkerchief.

"Ah seem to have given your rocker a bit of a kick," the man went on. "I assure you, suh, Ah meant no offense."

"None taken, sir, none taken at all," said Forebush, and stood immediately. This was a chance he couldn't afford to miss. He offered his hand. "I'm Matthew orebush." He left out the part about "Matthew" being an acronym made up by a flowery-headed mother, who'd christened him Marcus Aaron Timothy Thomas Hector Elijah Wordsworth Forebush. He could sort of understand most of it, many of the names belonging to uncles, but he'd be damned if he knew where the Wordsworth came from. "Pleased to welcome you to the town of Tucson."

The man took it, gave it a shake, and said, "Pleased to be welcomed and pleased to be met. Alfred Horatio Gant, at your service, suh."

Both men gave a courtly tip of the head, and Forebush pointed to the empty chair beside him. "Would you be inclined to sit for a spell, Mr. Gant, and bring a native of these uncivilized climes up to date? On the political atmosphere of the moment."

Gant studied the chair for a moment. "I believe I would, Mr. Forebush, suh," he answered, smiling wide. "I believe I would."

Franklin Q. Stubbins was dead. He had passed without once coming back to full consciousness and now lay, uncovered head to toe with old blankets and quilts, on Katie's dining table.

Fargo was outside, digging a grave through rock and sand on the far north side of the garden. Actually, it had taken him a while to find a place that could be dug down far enough, but he managed, and he was down nearly five feet. Good enough for Stubbins. Katie had wanted to stake him out for the birds to polish off, but Fargo wouldn't let her. If nothing else,

Stubbins had been white, and deserved to be buried that way. Maybe there wouldn't be a preacher, but at least there'd be a grave and a marker.

Well, at least there'd be a grave.

He stopped digging and shook himself off, the droplets of sweat scattering like river water off a hound dog, and then he climbed out of the grave. He figured to wait until sundown to bury Stubbins, just to be on the safe side. On several occasions, he'd seen snakebit men rise from the grave only half buried, and they tended to get really pissed once they figured out what was going on.

He figured you couldn't really blame them. He'd be a tad ticked off, too.

He went on up to the cave, drew himself a bucket of water, then went back outside before he stripped off his shirt and doused himself. He didn't believe that anything had ever felt as good as that cool water splashing over his sweat-drenched head and torso, and was about to go back inside for a second bucket when he heard approaching sounds over toward the eastern side of the mountain.

Quickly, he ducked inside. It could be Cuchillo Rojo, but then, it could be straggling survivors from the battle on the south side of the mountain, too. And he didn't like surprises.

But it was, in fact, Cuchillo Rojo, leading Stubbins' mule and wagon behind his horse. Fargo went out, raised a hand in greeting, and called Katie to come join him.

She ran past him and leapt into Cuchillo Rojo's arms before he was halfway to the man, and when he reached them, they were jabbering away in Apache. Once again, leaving Fargo out.

But when she saw him, she said in English, "Fargo, I told Cuchillo Rojo that Stubbins was dead in our kitchen, and that you'd just finished digging his grave.

I told him how brave you were, going up to the battle and everything!"

He smiled and shook his head. "Cuchillo Rojo's men were the brave ones."

Katie cut him off, adding, "Oh, I know! He said they were all dead, every single one, and only one of his men was killed."

Fargo made a sign with his fingers. "I mourn your loss, Cuchillo Rojo."

The warrior gestured back, and then in English said, "I thank you, Fargo." Then he turned toward Katie. "Take your mule," he said. "Take this mule, or my men will eat him."

Katie thanked him, then ran to lead the mule up and around to the front door. She cooed to it as she went, and Fargo noticed the mule's attitude picked up a good deal. Smart critter. A little of her cooing could pick up Fargo's spirits, too.

Since it appeared that Cuchillo Rojo was in the mood to speak English, Fargo asked a question. "You boys going to stick around awhile? In case they send reinforcements, I mean."

"We will stay until tomorrow, but no longer," the warrior answered. "It is time we move the camp again."

Fargo nodded, as if all his questions had been answered. They hadn't, of course, but when dealing with Apaches, you had to take what you could get. "We both thank you again, Cuchillo Rojo. You have done us, Daughter of Dancing Bird especially, a great service. We will not forget."

Cuchillo Rojo nodded. "Neither will we, Fargo."

That time, they both knew what he meant, but Fargo took no offense. He said, "Yes," and Cuchillo Rojo reined his horse away.

Fargo stood there, watching him until he disappeared around the side of the mountain's base, and then he turned back toward Katie. She had the mule stripped of his tack by then and was standing beside him, stroking him. "It's gonna be all right," he heard her say as he walked closer. "That nasty old Stubbins is gone, now, and he won't ever whip you again."

As if the mule understood, he bobbed his head up and down, rubbing it against Katie's front. She giggled and scratched him behind his long bay ears.

Fargo felt a little laugh bubble up his throat, too. He guessed that Stubbins' demise wasn't good news to just people. Even the animal kingdom was in on it.

"C'mon, Katie girl," he said. "Let's get old Stubbins put underground."

Her arms still ringing the mule's neck, she grinned wide and said, "Gladly!"

While Fargo tugged his shirt back on and prepared to drag Stubbins to his final rest, Matthew Forebush was just shaking hands with Alfred Gant—in the genteel Southern manner, of course—and making arrangements to meet with him on the morrow. Gant had associates who might be talked into a little work-for-silver, as well.

They parted company and went their separate ways—Forebush to his regular digs, out behind the Silver Slipper Saloon, and Gant to who-knew-where. Forebush hadn't asked him, and Gant hadn't told.

"He's probably stayin' at the Cactus Wren," Forebush muttered as he pushed his way through a knot of men, and kept on walking. "Someplace uppity like that." As men came out to light the gas lanterns along the streets, he came to an alley and made a left turn into it. He had to remember where the boxes, crates, and rubble were or he would have stepped or stumbled over them.

"Or maybe he's stoppin' at the Gold Rush," he added as he hung a right behind Lenny's Rooty-Toot and continued down the alley. "I'll bet that's it. The Gold Rush."

He would have liked to be staying at the Gold Rush. Oh, they had a floor show every night on a real stage, a nice dining room, a big fancy saloon that served champagne, and upstairs rooms for staying in or having a little fun with one of the girls from the bar.

When this war was over, then he'd be rich. Then he could stay at the Gold Rush all he wanted. Hell, he could buy the Gold Rush!

By the time he came, at last, to the back of the Silver Slipper, it was dark, and he returned the wave from one of his friends. There was a sort of informal camp there, a little place where out-of-work miners hung out, and hung their hats while they were in town. Forebush had found his first three men here. Now he had a fourth, which meant he needed only six more.

Only six, he thought as he moved toward his regular place against the wall, kicked open his bedroll and dropped down to it. *Just six more chumps to find . . .*

He was asleep almost before he lay all the way down.

Alfred Gant had reached his target, too, that being not the Gold Rush Hotel but Liddy's Boardinghouse. It was a step down from the Cactus Wren, but a site better than where Forebush was staying.

He checked into his room and had barely opened his satchel when there came a knock at the door. He opened it to find Harley Granger leaning against his doorway: not the Harley Granger that he knew and loved, but a Harley Granger dressed in rags and dust, and bearing a long red scratch across his forehead.

"The ladies back in Illinois would be disappointed in your attire, Harley," Gant said, any trace of a Southern drawl instantly erased. He opened the door wider. "Come on in. Make yourself at home."

10

Fargo shoveled the final spadeful of dirt over Stubbins and began piling the rocks on top into a sort of cairn. He planned to pull a picket off of what was left of the fence and use that for a marker, too. Stubbins must have done something good in his lousy life, even if only by accident.

Katie came out to help with the rocks, bringing a lit torch with her. It helped quite a bit. Dusk came early in the Sand Hills, as it was full of valleys and tall hills to block the sun.

Eventually they got the rocks in place, although not the marker, but Fargo made Katie stay while he said a few words over the grave. It was clear she wasn't enjoying herself—although he would have been concerned about anybody who had fun at a funeral—and when he said, "Amen," she fairly bolted back toward the cave, taking the torch with her.

She paused at the doorway and turned back to him, waving the torch. "Come on!" she called to him. "I made a special dinner!" And then she popped inside, leaving him to find his way back through the darkness.

While Forebush slept through dinnertime and Gant made do with a chicken sandwich provided by Harley Granger, Fargo found himself feasting on roasted partridge fresh from the oven, sage dressing, fresh peas, and canned peaches. It was the most satisfying meal he'd had in a long time, and he told Katie so.

"Glad you liked it," she purred, climbing into his lap and kissing his cheek.

He pulled her in closer. "This ain't bad, either."

She smiled and snuggled her head into the crook of his shoulder. "All with you in mind, Mr. Skye Fargo."

Softly, he grinned. The truth be told, he was damned tired, what with the staircase and the battle and Stubbins' burial and all. But he wasn't too tired to pass this up. He lifted her face and kissed her, long and hard.

Later, when they were on the floor in a nest of discarded clothing with their limbs entwined and their passions running hot, Fargo entered her suddenly, forcefully. She craned her head back, gasped for air to fuel her passion, and answered his thrust with one of her own, her hips moving like a pile driver over and around his steely manhood.

They went at each other as if no one had ever done this before, as if they were inventing it anew: no rules, no taboos, no rights or wrongs.

And when they were finally finished, when they both lay exhausted and spent, Fargo thought of his earlier vow and whispered, "Come to think of it, I'm buying *every* girl that's offered for sale to me from now on. Every last one."

He lifted his head just long and far enough to brush a kiss over Katie's sleeping brow, then fell back and, smiling, lapsed into a deep and dreamless sleep.

The next morning found Matt Forebush meeting Alfred Gant for breakfast at Molly's Over Easy. They both ordered the four-egg breakfast, and Gant began by telling Forebush that he thought he might be able to scrape four more men out of the woodwork—if Forebush thought he could handle that many more.

72

Forebush tamped down his inclination to shout, "Whoopee!" and ran his fingers through his mustache thoughtfully. "Reckon we could," he said. "Make the job go that much faster."

Gant nodded in agreement. "These gentlemen are here in Tucson, as fate would have it. It might take me a while to find them all, however."

"How long?"

Gant shrugged. "A day. Perhaps two."

Forebush nodded thoughtfully. "Sounds fine to me. And I thank you for your help, Alfred. These men, I trust, all know how to keep a confidence?"

Gant arched a brow. "They are all Southern gentlemen, suh, I assure you."

Forebush waved a hand. "Sorry. Didn't mean to be insulting. It's just that out here, I've run across so many—"

"It's all right, Matthew," Gant cut in. "I understand completely your need for secrecy, and your wish to keep it. You may put your trust in myself and my associates."

Forebush nodded and said, "Thank you, sir."

The breakfast came. Their eggs were accompanied by plates stacked with buttered toast, a half rasher of bacon for Gant and a pile of sausages for Forebush, plus a pot each of cactus, strawberry, and crabapple jelly.

Gant said, "When they serve you out here, they do not fool around."

Forebush laughed at the perplexed expression on his face, and Gant joined in after a moment.

Everything is gonna be fine, Forebush thought as he chortled around a bite of sausage, *just fine.*

The Apaches were gone.

Fargo, who had come upstairs on the hidden staircase once again, stood at the mouth of the tunnel, staring out over a pile of miners' bodies and what was left of a campsite. Naturally, the Apaches had taken all the guns and ammunition, anything they deemed of value, and all the horses.

But they hadn't burnt out the shafts, much to his surprise. He decided the bodies could wait, and lit a makeshift torch to lead him inside again. The second floor—the second to him and Katie, and the ground floor to miners coming in through the south-side entrance—was fairly nondescript, consisting of tunnels and more tunnels, some with rows of gunports carved into the stone and facing outward. None were large enough for a man to crawl through, but all were long enough to conceal a man pointing a rifle to the outside. The rifle, as well.

Up a winding staircase toward the southern entrance was the final floor: more tunnels with gunports, an ammunition alcove (now stripped of any ammo, thanks to their Apache saviors) and a large room with a desk and several chairs. Well, at least they hadn't torched it.

Fargo sat down behind the desk and began going through the drawers. Pencils, pens, paper, and petty cash were in the first one. The second was filled with correspondence from all quarters: mostly men high in the burgeoning Confederacy, and most inquiring as to how far the men had gotten. There was one half of a reply written to one Cornwallis R. Thibideaux, in which the writer had replied that his men were nearly finished with Part A of the dig, and planned on moving to Part B in the coming week. And that was all there was. Fargo couldn't help but wonder just what the hell Part B was. He figured that Part A was where he was sitting, but that didn't include an attack by Apache.

He smiled to himself a bit at that, then moved forward. The rest of the drawers turned up little of interest, save for a crude map of where the men had dug tunnels, and an answer to Part B: a proposed map of the tunnels in the north side of the mountain. They were to continue to just over Katie's cave-house.

He also found a diary, kept by the man he assumed had been in charge of the operation—one Augustus Bates. He thumbed through the yellowing pages, learning not much except that Bates mentioned Stubbins a few times—he brought them food and drink, it seemed, on occasion—and that if Bates had been Stubbins' mule, he would have kicked him to death long ago. Bates, it seemed, had been an animal lover. Or at least, an admirer of mules.

In the last drawer, he found another set of letters. These were all from a man named Matthew Forebush, and the most recent was dated nearly a year ago. Forebush, it seemed, was an ally of Bates', and planned to gather crews and bring them in every two weeks to spell Bates' men.

Fargo wondered how long this had been going on, and if Forebush was about to change the guard again. Once again, he returned to the diary and scanned for any references to Forebush's men having been there. Sure enough, there were. The big gaps between entries in the diary hadn't all been due to Bates' laziness. They had been partly due to the fact that Bates hadn't been there. Forebush had.

Fargo did a little more reading—and figuring—and determined that Forebush and his crew were due at the mountain in about six days. With the Apache long gone, it didn't leave him much time, choice, or leeway.

He had best figure out what to do, and figure it out in a large hurry.

It took him several hours to dig out a trough deep enough and long enough for the dead miners, and when he'd finished that, he went downstairs for a cool drink.

But Katie met him at the head of the stairs and handed over a tall glass and a pitcher of lemonade. He looked at her curiously, and she said, "You didn't see the trees growing to the right of the door?"

He shook his head no, and she said, "Well, they are partly hidden by rocks. These were the last of the lemons, so I hope they are fresh enough. I used the sugar Mama had left, and a little from your food bag."

They went out to the mouth of the tunnel to drink the lemonade, and neither one of them minded sharing the glass. The lemons had, indeed, been just right for making lemonade, and he told Katie so.

He also told her about the new shift of men who would be coming before the week was out.

Unaccountably, she burst into tears. "But they're supposed to be gone, Fargo!" she wept. "They're all supposed to be gone! Why can't they leave me in peace?"

He hugged her close and rocked her, and did everything he could think of to soothe her, but nothing worked. Finally, in exasperation, he said, "Katie, stop it! We've got to figure this out, and figure it out now!"

She lifted her tear-streaked face. "But how, Fargo? There is nothing we can do. Cuchillo Rojo is gone, and there are only two of us. You have only two guns. What is that against a gang of miners?"

Fargo didn't admit as much, but she had a point. What could he be expected to do against a few dozen rifles and sidearms? After all, he didn't know how many men Forebush would be bringing. Ten? Twenty? Fifty?

He had a sinking feeling in the pit of his stomach. Any way he looked at it, they'd be outnumbered and outgunned.

He said, "I know, Katie, I know. I'm thinkin' that we'd best get our butts out of here and into town."

But what he had thought would be a comforting

reply only drove her to deeper weeping. "No, no," she wailed. "My father's silver mine. It's all I have left. Don't you understand? It's everything! Can't you understand, Fargo? I don't have to live out my life as somebody's hired squaw!"

"It's all right, baby," he said, hugging her closer and rocking her gently. "We'll figure out something. We'll figure out a way."

As to just what that way might be, he had not the first clue. But at least it soothed her tears a little.

At long last, her weeping trailed off enough that she lifted her face and whispered, "But how, Fargo? How can you possibly imagine you can hold off so many men? I know you are a mighty warrior, but even the great Cuchillo Rojo could not hold off so many by himself, even if he had his squaw by his side, and even if Glows Like Sun knew how to use a gun."

Fargo didn't know how to answer her, but he was beginning to get the seed of an idea.

He took a last gulp of lemonade, then climbed to his feet to stare out over the unburied bodies of the former miners. The trench was dug, but they weren't in it yet. And they weren't going to be anytime soon if he had his way about it.

He pulled Katie to her feet and pointed to the campfire, or what was left of it. "Go build me a decent circle of rocks. Indian style. I want it to look as if Cuchillo Rojo's men reset the camp after they trashed it."

She looked at him oddly, as if he'd suddenly lost his mind.

"Just do it, Katie," he said. "And if they make any special signs around a cooking fire, do that, too. Make it look like they're comin' back." He took a last look around before he went inside to retrieve any papers that might be important later, and to set fire to whatever in the tunnels would burn.

11

Three, so far.

That's what Forebush kept telling himself. Gant had taken him to meet two more Southern fellows who could keep their mouths shut and were willing to work for the silver they found, and they'd all agreed to help with the mine. Now they were on their way to meet the fourth.

He and Gant entered the Cactus Wren Hotel. It wasn't as fancy as the Gold Rush, but it would do. The man at the desk directed them to Room 15, which they found after going down a long hallway lit by copious lanterns and lamps.

Gant knocked at the door, an odd little series of coded knocks, and soon the door was opened by a tall, skinny man with long, narrow sideburns and a pencil-thin mustache. At first glance, his brocade vest made him look like a riverboat gambler, but it didn't take Forebush very long to slide him into the Southern Gentleman category.

"Good afternoon, Mistah Gant," he said while glancing over at Forebush. "I see you've brought me some company."

"Indeed I have, suh," Gant replied. "Allow me to introduce Mr. Matthew Forebush. Matthew, meet my friend, Mistah Cronus Reckenthaller."

Forebush and Reckenthaller shook hands. He had a firm handshake, Forebush thought.

"Gentlemen, won't you enter?" Reckenthaller said as he bowed curtly and stepped aside.

Inside of a half hour, Forebush had laid the plan out while Reckenthaller nodded and Gant egged him on. And in the end, he agreed to the plan. Or at least, part of it.

"How much silver has your average man taken out of this mine, Mistah Forebush? In, say, a week's time," Reckenthaller asked.

"Not exactly certain, Mr. Reckenthaller. And please, call me Matthew."

He nodded. "Matthew," Reckenthaller repeated. "And you will please address me as Cronus."

"Thank you, Cronus," Forebush said with a smile. "Now, what the boys have been doing in the past is to pool all the ore they find together, truck it here to town, and split up what the assayer pays them. I reckon it's been about thirty dollars a week per man, more or less. How's that sound to you?"

Reckenthaller scratched his chin thoughtfully. "I suppose it will have to do," he said. "More important," he added, "is the everlasting glory of the South."

All three men raised their glasses to that, and drank deep.

"The everlasting glory of the South," repeated Gant.

"To the everlasting glory of the South," echoed Forebush, and added, "Long may she reign."

While Fargo was inside, seeing to his papers and his fire, Katie finished staging the campsite, then considered her options. She could go along with Fargo, but she didn't see much sense in his plan. Most whites knew very little about Indians, let alone whether they had set a camp up to return to it. She knew all her work had been in vain, but she'd done it to make Fargo happy. And now she was thinking of trying something that would not make him happy at all.

She drummed her fingers against her side for a moment. Then, her mind set, she began to climb up the side of the mountain. She would rather have clambered up to the top of one of the sandhills all around, but they were not high enough. She could do better here, even if she couldn't gain the summit.

When she had gone up as far as she could—which was still higher than the sand hills—she built a fire, which she lit with a kitchen match she had shoved into her skirt pocket. Once the fire was lit, she added fresh weeds and grass to make smoke. She then began to fan the fire with her skirts.

She could only hope that Cuchillo Rojo had not moved too far away to see her signals.

She was back down the mountain before Fargo came outside, and was able to explain her ripped skirt—which she had snagged and torn coming down—by blaming the surrounding cactus.

He hadn't set fire to the side tunnel leading to their quarters, he explained, and so they went back down to their rooms by the short route. Katie hadn't seen hide nor hair of any signal from Cuchillo Rojo, so she had to assume that he'd moved his people too far, or at least out of sight of the southern skies. As for Fargo, his arms were filled with papers and some books from the shelves. He'd left most of them to burn, seeing as they were useless to him—or anyone else he could think of.

He'd kept the diary and a few ledgers as well as most of the letters, along with the pens and pencils from the desk. He figured that a person could never have enough of those.

"You get your signals sent?" Fargo asked when they were halfway down the stairs.

Katie started. "I beg your pardon?"

"Your smoke signals. Did you get them all sent off?" He was walking ahead of her, and allowed himself a smirk.

Katie paused a moment, thinking what to say, but finally burst out with, "Yes, Mr. Snooping Hound, I did."

He smiled. "Any reply?"

After a moment, she said, "No."

"Didn't think so," he said as he came to the bottom of the staircase and opened the latch, swinging the door open into Katie's old room.

They trooped from the stairway, Fargo swinging the door closed behind them. Katie, carrying the pitcher and glass, was already on her way to the kitchen when he turned around. He supposed he'd embarrassed her, asking about the smoke signals she'd sent. She probably didn't realize that her skin and clothing smelled of smoke, and that her face was smudged with traces of it.

Oh, well. Nothing a little water wouldn't take care of.

And secretly, he was glad she'd tried to contact Cuchillo Rojo, even though the chances were slim to none that he'd come to their aid once again. A hawk might shit in your palm once, but he surely wouldn't bet on the same hawk doing it twice in the same day.

He found himself glancing up, just to make sure there wasn't a hawk in the room about to prove him wrong.

There wasn't, so he followed Katie out to the kitchen. He walked up behind her as she was putting the glass away, and put his arms around her. Immediately, all the mad went out of her and she slouched back against him. "Your daddy build in anything like a bathtub in this place?" he asked.

"No," she said with a smile in her voice. "But he bought one."

"Oh, he did, did he?" Fargo said and turned her so that she was facing him. "And whereabouts did he hide it?"

She grinned wider. "If you take two steps to the side, you'll be standing in it." When Fargo wrinkled his brow, she laughed and said, "Under the table, silly!"

He bent and looked, and sure enough, there was a bathtub beneath the table, complete with claw-feet. He hadn't seen it before because of the tablecloth's droop, and he slapped himself on the forehead.

Katie giggled, and he said, "If it'd been a bear, we'd both be goners!"

She pursed her lips and tried to look parental. "Fargo, if it had been a bear, I would have told you long ago."

"Oh, that makes me feel a helluva lot better, Katie."

She said, "Why do you ask that, anyway?" She began to rub his arm. "You want to take a bath? You want to watch me take a bath?" She wiggled her eyebrows.

He chuckled and held her closer. "How about both at the same time?"

She stood on tiptoes and kissed the line of his jaw, just to one side of his chin, then pulled away. "Help me move the table," she said, and went to the far end. He followed her lead, and soon the bathtub stood alone in the center of the room.

She stoked the stove and put several vessels of water on to heat, then pulled a bucket from beneath the sink and filled it from the pump. "This will take a little while," she said, grinning. "Can you wait that long?"

"Watching you makes the waiting worthwhile," Fargo replied, and took a seat on the battered sofa, where he proceeded to pull off his boots.

The bath was soon ready, with its temperature adjusted to please Katie, and just as quickly they were both naked and in the water. Katie sat between Fargo's legs, with her back toward him, and he insisted she wash her hair. The smoky smell was strongest in it.

She lathered it, combed it while it was soapy, then rinsed and rinsed and rinsed it. It glistened blue-black in the darkening kitchen. Fargo had washed his hair and face and beard while she was doing her hair, and when she finally stopped rinsing, he took the soap from her, lathered up both hands generously, and reached around her to take a breast in each one.

She let out a little giggle of a squeal at the initial surprise of it, then relaxed back into him as he lathered away. And he soaped every full bulge of breast, every crevice of nipple three times over.

Next he moved to her neck and upper chest, then to her shoulders and underarms, creaming her in suds, then down her stomach and ribs to her belly, then farther down, to her secret portal. He ran his fingers through the hair there, washing her between her legs as if he were polishing a shine while tiny little chirps of pleasure rose up her throat.

When she began to squirm against his soapy fingers too strongly, he pushed her forward and began to soap her back. It was such a pretty back, muscular yet feminine, nipped and tucked in all the right places. And then he slid the bar of soap lower, over, then between her buttocks.

He heard her moan, "Fargo . . ." but he kept on scrubbing until he had gone as far as he could reach down her thighs.

"Afraid you're gonna have to take over, darlin'," he said as he ran the soap over his own chest. "I can't reach those pretty calves of yours."

"I'd say you'd reached about enough," she replied, and suddenly she was facing him, sitting cross-legged between his thighs. She snatched the soap from his hands. "My turn," she purred, and began to lather him.

By the time she'd soaped his chest, his shoulders, his arms, and abdomen and made her way down to the furry patch at the juncture of his legs, he was too far gone to tell her to wait, let alone stop. She took his member into her soapy hands and began to massage it gently up and down even as it grew. Soon she was stroking it with one hand while her other was massaging his balls and running soap deep between his legs.

With his last available ounce of dignity—and good sense—Fargo blurted out, "No, wait, honey!"

She did immediately. "I was doing something wrong?"

"No," he said after he took a couple of deep breaths. "You were doin' everything just right." She reached for him again, but he blocked her hands. "Hold on, baby. Just wait. Now, rinse yourself off as best you can." The water was thick with dirt and soap residue, but he had an idea.

When they were both reasonably rinsed, he helped her, naked and dripping, from the tub, then had her bend over the sink while he poured the last of the warm water from the stove over her raven's wing hair. Then he wrapped her hair up in a towel before he grabbed one and applied it to his own back. Once he'd tied it around his waist, he picked up his buckskins and tossed them in the bathwater, then picked up her dress and threw it in, too.

"What—?" she said, surprised.

"Gonna let 'em soak for a while, Katie. We've got other things to do."

Then he swept her up, naked as she was except for the towel on her head, and carried her to the sofa. He laid her on the towels he'd left there, dropped his own towel, and settled between her legs, entering her almost immediately.

She was more than ready for it, and began to kiss him the second he was close enough. Her hands fluttered like captive moths over his back and shoulders, and her thighs, still wet from the bath, slid up and down his sides.

He lowered his mouth to her nipple and began to suckle her even as he intensified his thrusting. He felt the power of lightning surge through him as she met every thrust, countered every parry, and he felt that each time he went deeper, uncovered new territory.

And then suddenly he felt himself taking that steep train to the stairs. He felt himself rising, rising, then coming explosively, thrusting twice more, then collapsing on Katie's shoulder.

He became aware of a thrumming sensation coming from inside her, and knew he'd satisfied her, too, although he was stumped as to when. All he knew was that he had never come so damned hard in his life.

He lifted his head and looked into her eyes. "Aw, Katie," he breathed, and kissed her.

12

That evening found Cuchillo Rojo clustered about the evening fire with several of his top braves. They had been in conference for some time.

"We cannot return," repeated Soaring Hawk adamantly, in Apache. "It is too far to go when we have to move the camp tomorrow at first light."

"And when we have been there already," added Rearing Horse. "We have given aid once. Once should be enough."

"We would be mad to consider it," said the normally quiet Racing Moon.

A new voice, a feminine one, joined the conversation. "And you would be mad to ignore her cry for help," said Glows Like Sun. She stood in back of her husband, Cuchillo Rojo, until he gave her a sign to come sit beside him. "She would not ask you such a favor if it were not important."

Cuchillo Rojo nodded at this, then fell into a deep ponder. At last, he said, "Her smoke said they would not come for at least three or four more days. We have time to move the camp, Soaring Hawk."

"Our ponies are tired," Soaring Hawk said immediately.

"Less tired than they will be in three days," replied Cuchillo Rojo.

Glows Like Sun nodded her agreement, her long

flaxen hair moving as she did so. "Am I not right that you will have the element of surprise on your side if you get back to the mountain before they do?"

"She has spoken the truth," said Cuchillo Rojo, and pursed his lips. "The mother of my son is wise once again, and I have decided. We will move camp tomorrow and use the following day to settle in. Then, the day after that, we will go back to Stone Mountain and the home of Daughter of Dancing Bird, and we will see what can be done to help her. Is it so?"

In unison, although without as much enthusiasm as Cuchillo Rojo would have liked, the three other braves answered, "It is so, my chief."

Glows Like Sun softly added, "The gods will make it so."

In Tucson, Forebush, Gant, and Reckenthaller were just finishing dinner at the Gold Rush Restaurant. Reckenthaller had announced early on that he was paying, which came as a great relief to Forebush, who didn't have two dimes to rub together. They'd had beefsteaks all around with all the trimmings, and were now sipping coffee and smoking cigars over a cleared table.

"When do you expect we'll be moving out?" asked Cronus Reckenthaller, who, as the only one to have ordered dessert, was dallying over a slice of pecan pie. "Ah, for one, am anxious to get this operation under way."

Gant held up a finger. "Now, Cronus, Ah do believe that Mr. Forebush, here, is in charge of the operation, and he has associates to consult with."

"True, true," said Forebush. He'd given it a great deal of thought, and figured that even if he didn't have as many bodies as they'd originally asked for, the ones he had were worth two apiece. Well, one and a half, anyway.

They'd do just fine. Besides, he'd scoured Tucson with a fine-tooth comb and could find no one else who gave a damn about the North or the South. They were more concerned about the Apache menace or Mexican raiders or water rights.

He'd be just fine with the men he had.

"I imagine that I'll be hearing from my associates in the next day or so. Then we'll troop on out to the mine," he said.

His two dinner companions nodded.

"Will Ah need my own saddle horse," Gant asked, "or will you supply mounts?"

"I'd say yes, you'd need to furnish your own," Forebush replied. "If they come back with the buckboard, you could ride out in that, but it'll be full of ore on the way back. I don't think either of you gentlemen are prepared to walk up and down the Santa Ritas."

Gant nodded, and Reckenthaller muttered, "Ah see. . . ."

Forebush quickly saved the situation by saying, "Now, there are some canny horse traders in this town. If you gentlemen would like, I could take you around to meet some of the fair bargainers. Save you some cash as well as heartbreak."

Both Gant and Reckenthaller nodded. "That would be most gentlemanly of you, suh," Reckenthaller said, and finished his pie.

"Indeed it would," said Gant. "Your aid would be most appreciated."

"Good," said Forebush, and raised his wineglass. "We'll meet out front of Mr. Reckenthaller's place of residence tomorrow at ten, then?"

Reckenthaller, too, raised his glass. "The Cactus Wren at ten of the morning, gentlemen."

Gant lifted his glass as well. "The Cactus Wren at ten it is." He drank deeply, draining the glass dry.

* * *

Although it had grown late, Fargo left Katie to drowse while he saw to the Ovaro. The stud was restless in his "stall," pushing the mule around and nipping at him. It was unusual behavior for him.

Fargo found the mule backed into a corner and the Ovaro about to lash out at him with both hind hooves. He said, "Hey, buddy, watch what you're doin'," and the stud stopped in midstride, choosing to instead wander over and nuzzle Fargo's hands.

Fargo, shaking his head, gently pushed him aside. "You really think you deserve a treat, you old bully, you?" Just to be gnarly, the stallion bobbed his head up and down a few times, then rested his chin on Fargo's shoulder and let out a long sigh.

Fargo laughed in spite of himself. "You old pirate," he said. "Let me check the kitchen." He would have checked his pockets, but all his clothes were hung out on the wash line in the kitchen, probably still dripping.

He made his way to the kitchen, blind and naked, and finally managed to locate his grub bag and its supply of sugar cubes. He took enough for the Ovaro and the mule, too, and then felt his way back to the bedroom acting as a stable. The Ovaro was waiting for him at the doorway, but the mule was still hiding in the corner. He let himself in, offered a sugar lump to the Ovaro, then made his way over to the mule, with the Ovaro, still crunching sugar, on his heels. He offered sugar to the mule, who hesitated a moment before taking it, as if he were afraid the Ovaro would snatch it away before he had a chance.

Fargo kept on giving them sugar—first one, then the other—until his supply was depleted. Then he patted them both on the neck, said, "Now, play nice, boys," and exited the room.

The moon was full and lit the garden wonderfully, and he took a moment to walk down the front hallway and stare out at it a moment. But something was wrong. He couldn't figure out what, at first. Everything he looked at seemed to be right, and what it ought to be. But then he finally looked out toward Stubbins' grave.

It was all wrong. The dirt wasn't the same way he'd packed it down, and there was a bulge of dirt on the far end, the end where Stubbins' head should be. Still naked, he walked outside and stood over the grave.

The level of dirt was down by a foot or so, and there was an opening at the head end. He could see the traces where a body had pulled itself out.

He was gripped by chills that had nothing to do with the cool night air.

He ran to the outside pump, and sure enough, there was a little water there that hadn't evaporated yet, water that showed the pump had been used, probably late this afternoon.

Damn! How could he have buried somebody alive? That was the first thing that crossed his mind. How on earth could Stubbins not have shown any pulse, any heartbeat that he could detect? And how could he have dug himself out?

He hadn't been able to bury the corpse as deeply as he would have wished, but Stubbins still would have had to dig himself out from under at least four feet of ground.

And where was he now? That was the big question. Fargo knew he wasn't armed. He had taken Stubbins' weapons before the burial and removed them to the kitchen. But he could be out there anywhere, lurking. Most likely, he'd gone back up around the mountainside while he and Katie were up there, tending to the site.

"Well, don't make yourself too goddamn comfortable, you scrofulous sonofabitch," Fargo muttered between clenched teeth, and cut back inside, pulling his damp clothes off the line and climbing back into them. This time somebody was going to be good and dead.

He hoped it would be Stubbins.

The next thing he did was to check Katie's old room. There was no sign that anyone had passed through it, and he dragged the heavy bed over in front of the stone passage's door to make certain no one could go up. Or come down.

Next, he woke Katie and whispered their situation to her. Her expression quickly changed from delight at seeing his face to terror as he spoke and quickly told her the facts. He handed her his knife and tucked her away in the far corner of the kitchen, checked his sidearm, grabbed his rifle, and left. He had to go up on foot. The Ovaro would make too much noise.

He realized when he was halfway around the mountain's base that it must have been the sounds of Stubbins moving above them that had stirred up the paint stallion and the mule.

Slowly, he made his way around the mountain, and when he came in sight of the clearing where the camp had been, and where the bodies were now piled, he stopped, crouched, and studied the area closely. Other than a pair of coyotes scavenging the body pile, there was nothing moving. Stubbins must be inside.

Slowly, soundlessly, Fargo crept toward the shaft's mouth, listening at every juncture for sound from within the tunnel. There was nothing. At least, until he had broached the tunnel's mouth.

Suddenly and with no warning, Stubbins came out of nowhere, blindsiding Fargo and shoving him outside with Stubbins on top, landing blow after blow to Fargo's midsection.

Fargo automatically shoved the smaller man off him, although his ribs had taken quite a pummeling, and rolled away while reaching for his sidearm. He pulled it and aimed at the place where Stubbins should have been, but his quickly fired shot hit nothing but air and rock.

Swearing under his breath, he quickly scanned the area, but could see neither hide nor hair of Stubbins. He gave the area a second, closer look. Finally, satisfied that nobody was outside but himself, he quietly got to his feet and started toward the tunnel again.

This time, no one came barreling at him, and he quickly entered the tunnel despite the pain in his rib cage. He wouldn't be surprised if Stubbins had cracked a few of his ribs, the dumb bastard.

It was dark inside, but he didn't want to light a match. That would give him away immediately. His gun drawn, he began inching along the tunnel wall, taking a path that would lead him to the secret staircase. He'd have bet money that Stubbins had gone that way, since he now knew that Fargo was up here.

Slowly, Fargo worked his way along the tunnel, listening constantly for any sign of Stubbins. But there was none to be heard. If men had said that there was no harder man to kill than Fargo, then he decided Stubbins had him beat, hands down. On top of clawing his way out of the grave, the sonofabitch could turn into vapor.

Fargo made the several turns to the final straightaway to the storage closet and the stairway, and there he paused. He could just catch a small scratching sound, the sound of a man trying to quietly unlatch the top staircase door with no light to see by.

Fargo felt better, but not by much. He didn't trust Stubbins not to have a knife, or to have secreted a gun somewhere up here. Or to have one of his pet rattlers in his pocket. But he moved forward, silently, anyway.

He inched closer to the storage closet door. The scratching sounds were louder now, and definitely came from within. Fargo was about to put his hand on the latching mechanism when the scratching stopped abruptly.

On moccasin-clad feet, he quickly and silently moved to the side. And waited.

It took Stubbins a full three minutes to thread his way back through the closet and find the latch of the door, and another two minutes to open it. But at last he did, and Fargo, waiting outside, wasted no time.

He waited for the dim outline of Stubbins to emerge from the closet, fired once, heard Stubbins fall with a dull thud, then fired again. He was taking no chances this time.

He waited, listening for the sounds of breathing or a twitching hand, but none came, and at last he lit a match. Stubbins lay on the floor amid the rat droppings, dead as a fried carp. Fargo kicked him to make certain, then kicked him again just to make *absolutely* certain he was dead, and only then did he holster his weapon.

When he turned the body over, he found that his first shot had gone straight through Stubbins' heart, and the second had gone through his belly.

He gave the body another kick, then grabbed the corpse's arm and began to drag it outside through the tunnel. One more to toss on the pile.

He did, and after he did, he glared at the corpse, saying, "Now stay dead this time, or else!"

13

Forebush sat crouched on his bedroll behind the saloon, thinking what his next possibilities were. He had his men—not as many as he'd wanted, but enough to see him through—and now all he needed was transport. Tomorrow morning, Bates should arrive with a freight wagon full of ore and a passel of tired men. Then it would be Forebush's turn to head over the Santa Ritas with the new crew and dig out some more of the mountain. It would truly be a wonder to behold when they were finished, an unbreachable fortress. It was too bad, he thought, that the terrain to the east was so different; the South would be unstoppable if they had a few more of these fortresses.

Gant, too, was awake and thinking, although his thoughts were far from Forebush's. He and Reckenthaller had been sent ahead, from Washington, D.C., on a special assignment, and on direct presidential orders. They were to infiltrate Bates' and Forebush's operation, and put an end to it if possible. Lincoln was aware of Mexico's forays into the U.S. and didn't want them siding with the South simply to gain a foothold on U.S. territory. In addition, although no one suspected that the war would reach as far west as

Arizona, no one wanted to take a chance that it would.

The other men Gant had taken Forebush to recruit were in on it, too, and each one would do his utmost to uphold the sovereignty of his country. Of this, Gant was certain.

He wouldn't have recommended them for this operation if he weren't sure.

The one man that Gant would have given his eyeteeth to have along on this mission was one Skye Fargo, otherwise known as the Trailsman, who had been handy before on covert operations. He was friendly—or, at least, on speaking terms—with most tribes of the natives, knew his way around the countryside, and was friendly with the locals.

The only trouble was, you never knew just where he was. For all Gant knew, Fargo could be up high in the Rockies, taking the sun in California, down Texas way, or even paddle-wheeling down the Mississippi.

He wished Fargo were here, though.

Meanwhile, Fargo was having a serious talk with Katie. He'd explained that he'd thought it over six or seven ways, and the only thing he could think to do was to go to town and seek help there. Surely he could find enough Northern sympathizers to help him run these claim thieves off.

But Katie would have none of it. "This is my place," she claimed time after time. "I belong here. No Southern thieves are going to run me off of it."

No matter what, he couldn't move her, not even an inch.

And so he was stuck. He said, "You're not giving me much choice, Katie, my love. We stay here, we're going to die. I don't particularly want to die. Do you?"

But she didn't fall for it. She said, "I want to stay

here and fight. With or without you." And that, as they say, was that.

He folded his arms across his chest. She was being impossible. He supposed he could just haul off and slug her, toss her in the wagon's bed, and deal with her when she woke up, somewhere in the Santa Ritas. But he couldn't hit a woman, especially the woman who'd given him the night before. He slouched back and pulled his hat down over his eyes, trying to decide if that night with Katie had been good enough to die for.

It didn't take him long. It hadn't been. Nothing was that good. He got to his feet.

"Katie," he said, "you're a oner. But I'll be damned if I'll die for you. I'm sorry, but that's the way it is. I'll stick around for the rest of today, but come tomorrow morning, I'm gone."

Her face fell as suddenly as a cake in range of a slamming door, and suddenly, she was crying. No, not just crying, but bellowing and pleading and weeping buckets and begging him to reconsider, to stay, to help her.

But Fargo could be stubborn, too. He was tempted, but he held fast to his decision. There was no way he was going to willingly lay down his life against overwhelming odds when he could take a ride to town, have an honest-to-God beer, and ride back out here with plenty of reinforcements.

So he said, "No, Katie. I'll try to get back in time. If they come, just hide yourself away. Hide the door of this house with brush and debris. Your best bet is to pull the table back in place, then climb into the bathtub. You got that, honey? And leave the door up to the mine blocked."

Reluctantly she nodded, but she didn't break down and offer to come to town with him. Damnit.

"Chances are that they'll be so took up with the

results of the Indian attack that they won't even think to look around this side," he added hopefully.

She looked up at him, as sober as a judge, and said, "From your lips to God's ears, Fargo."

During the middle of the afternoon, Forebush had slipped away from town and ridden up into the Santa Ritas. He went to the usual place, where he knew his smoke signals could be easily read by the men at the mountain, and built himself a smoky little fire. Just enough burning wood, just enough green. And when it was ready, he began to signal, in Morse code, "We are ready. We are ready. Come now? Come now?"

He signaled them six times over, and was perplexed when he received no answer. He waited a few minutes, then started all over again, wondering what the hell Bates was doing to keep him—or his men—from seeing the signals. It was a windless day, and therefore he couldn't chalk it up to the weather. The signals were rising high and clear, about the best he'd ever seen them.

But still, there was no answer, neither were there any signs—in the form of errant smoke—of anybody building a fire to answer him.

Shaking his head, he gave up and put out his fire. It was nearing sundown, and he didn't want to try to navigate his way down the mountains by memory and moonlight. There was nothing for it but to take what few men he had out there in the morning and hope for the best. And also hope to God that it wasn't Apaches.

Fargo spent a restless night.

Every little sound that echoed down from up above, he took for signs of more miners. But when he proved himself wrong, he was still sure it was them at every new sound.

97

Nothing seemed to bother Katie. She slept like a log through the whole night. Fargo wondered if she was just naturally that unconcerned, or if knowing that he was there had anything to do with it. It didn't really matter, he supposed. Nothing really mattered at this point.

At dawn, he saddled the Ovaro. "Gonna have to do some mountain climbing, old man," he muttered as he cinched the girth. "Our days of leisure are over, I'm afraid."

He led the stud out into the front hallway after barricading the stall door behind him to keep the mule in. He was just taking down the barricade at the front door when someone cleared their throat behind him.

It was Katie. She came around the Ovaro and threw her arms around Fargo. "You must go." She said it with finality, as if her fate was sealed and nothing could change it.

"Yes," replied Fargo. "I must. It's the only hope I have of finding men and getting back here in time, Katie."

She nodded. "I understand." A tear formed at the corner of her eye, and she stepped back, releasing him. "God be with you, Fargo. Go in peace."

She was certainly being a lot nicer—and calmer—about this thing than he had expected. He began to have second thoughts but suddenly stopped himself. The only prayer they had of saving themselves would be to stick to his plan. Period.

He went back to clearing the doorway, and when he'd finished, he returned to Katie, who had been watching from the back, and kissed her long and hard. She returned it hungrily, but there was no demand in it, implicit or otherwise. He knew then that she had reconciled herself to his leaving.

And that she would stay.

He led the Ovaro outside and mounted up while

98

she rebarricaded the door, and when she had done it to his satisfaction, he turned the Ovaro east, toward the Santa Ritas and Tucson, on the other side. He prayed only that he could find enough men, and that they could get there in time.

After a half hour had passed, he had left the Sand Hills behind and began the long climb up the Santa Ritas. The problem was not that they were so high, but that the terrain was so rugged and rocky. Very few times did he come to a strip of clear path going up, and many times even one of those would lead him to a sheer wall of stone that he'd have to figure a way around.

It wasn't a pleasant ride.

It was tough on the Ovaro, too, and every few minutes he had to stop and let the horse have a breather.

But at last, after riding half a day, he found that he had crested the range. He climbed down off his stallion and gave him a welcome pat on the neck. "It's all downhill from here, boy," he said as he dug into his grub bag for some sugar. The horse devoured it greedily.

He took a long drink of water from his canteen, then poured some into his cupped hand and offered it to the horse. It went down faster than the sugar had, and he repeated the procedure. "That's all for now, buddy," he said, corking the water. "You've gotta wait until we get down the other side. Don't look that far, does it?"

Indeed, it didn't. But then again, it was a short way as the crow flew. And he and the Ovaro were no birds. Between them, they had to deal with six legs. He found himself wishing that the Ovaro could suddenly turn into Pegasus.

No such luck, though, and he remounted once he'd figured the best way to start the downward journey. He showed the Ovaro a little heel and said, "Let's get on with it, then."

14

In Tucson, Forebush had been up with the dawn, too. He'd had all his men rounded up and ready to ride by eight thirty, and they cut out of town at a little before nine. They took the southern route over the Santa Ritas, which Fargo would have much preferred if only he'd known about it. The trail had originally been blazed by Katie Dugan's father, and then many years later, widened and smoothed by the men who dug the silver and excavated the fortress.

Forebush made good time, and he also studied his newest recruits as they went. Of the four newest, one in particular rode his mount with a military stiffness that he tried not in the least to hide.

The other rode slouched—normal, thought Forebush— but every once in a while he tapped the place where his scabbard would be, if he had one. Which, of course, he didn't. Only military men rode with swords.

Gant rode upright and proud, as Forebush would have expected a gentleman to ride his mount, and Reckenthaller simply sat the saddle and went along. Nothing fancy there, just a cowpoke's seat.

The other men were a nondescript bunch. Old, young, and everything in between. He hadn't told them about the unreturned smoke signals he'd sent the last afternoon. That would have to wait until they got a bit closer, until he figured that they wouldn't want to turn around. Well, or figured they were too far into the deal to back out without looking like a bunch of pantywaists.

They were nearing the crest of the peak that would start them downward, toward their goal in the sand hills. They didn't have to travel all the way up to the peak, but Forebush always thought of it that way. It was easier than "the mountain where you pass through three high valleys and a stone canyon on your way to the other side."

Forebush was all for the easiest way to do things.

And so, when he saw the rider in the distance, the first thing he thought was to pull his rifle. After all, the horse was easier to see than the man atop him, and the horse himself was an Indian paint. He figured it was an Apache.

But to his right, Gant shot out a hand and said, "Hold on, suh!"

Forebush was angry, but he didn't shoot. He snarled, "What if that's an Apache, Gant? Ain't you read a newspaper since you been out here?"

Gant was squinting into the distance. "That's no Apache, suh. I do believe that's my good friend Skye Fargo, on his Ovaro stud. I have always greatly admired that horse."

Forebush raised the rifle to his shoulder again. "How bad you want him?" he asked with a grin.

Gant grimaced. "Do not fire that rifle, Mr. Forebush, or I shall have to take action." He looked like he could do it, too.

Forebush let the rifle drop and, a little nervously, said, "Can't you take a joke, Gant?"

"Not when it concerns the life of a friend."

Gant stared at him, deadly serious, so Forebush shrugged and stuck his rifle back in its boot, silently telling himself, *There's always next time, buddy.*

Gant seemed happy, now, but still Forebush was relieved when, after asking him and the others to wait, he excused himself and rode toward the faraway figure, hollering and waving his arm.

Fargo, if that was whoever the hell he was, whoaed his paint and sat there, head cocked, waiting for Gant to catch up with him. This was about the same time that Forebush noticed that this "Fargo" wore buckskins, like an Indian.

But he seemed to have a beard, too.

Forebush shrugged. Well, maybe Gant did know the man. And maybe he was white. Seemed like one helluva small world, though.

Gant rode up to Fargo at a fast trot—the fastest he dared push the horse on this terrain—still waving his arm and hoping to hell that Fargo wouldn't shoot first and ask questions later at the sound of his Southern accent. He wasn't any too sure of it himself, and had to be careful choosing his words around Forebush.

Fortunately, Fargo had recognized him and called out, "Gant!" before he was all the way there. He was suddenly very happy that he'd chosen to use his real name on this mission.

"Fargo!" he called back, and when he reached him, leapt off his mount before it had stopped all the way. Fargo was on the ground by then, too, and the two men threw their arms about each other like long-lost brothers.

"Gant, you crazy old sonofabitch!" Fargo cried, finally releasing him—at least, to arm's length. "What the hell are you doing out here in Arizona, in the middle of goddamn nowhere? Can't they find you work in Washington these days?"

"Yes, they can, but it's all out here these days,"

Gant said cryptically. Fargo looked at him oddly, and Gant explained as quickly as he could, all the time keeping his back toward the far-off Forebush.

"See, we got information that the Southern forces were planning to broaden the fight to the west coast," he began, and kept on talking until he came to the part where he and three friends from his bureau were sent west to troll for Southern sympathizers. "And I landed one—the right one—first thing off the bat. Forebush and his friends. Got him to enlist my three buddies, too. We're on our way to—"

Fargo held up his hands. "Hold it. I know where you're going."

Gant cocked a brow. "You do?"

After they'd spent another five minutes telling and listening, Fargo said, "Here comes Forebush right now." He raised a hand, plastered a grin on his face, and waved.

Gant followed suit, and Forebush waved back.

"Come with us," Gant said softly. "Help us."

"Sure thing," Fargo said loudly. "Happy to." And added, more softly, "Be real pleased to, as a matter of fact. Oh, your plan was to do something to trip these fellas up so they'll land on their faces, right?"

"Right," replied Gant somewhat curiously.

"Perfect!" beamed Fargo, who then walked out to the approaching Forebush.

Forebush got down off his mount and waited for Fargo to reach him, then greeted him with an out-held hand. "Fargo, is that you? Gant was just saying how you always rode that big painted horse."

Fargo smiled and shook hands. "Right. The Ovaro." He heard the horse snort at the mention of his name, and turned to find that Gant had followed, leading both their mounts behind him.

"Found you another man, suh!" Gant said, and

Fargo was surprised by the accent once again. "Fargo, here, would be more'n happy to do a little diggin' for all the ore he picks out. Right, Fargo?"

"Uh, sure! That's right, Gant," Fargo said. They hadn't gotten to the specifics of the deal yet, so what Forebush and Gant were telling him now was news to him.

"Well, c'mon along, gents," Forebush said as he stepped back up on his mount. "We've got a lot of digging to do. You know, Fargo, I'm more than pleased to finally meet up with you. Been hearing stories about 'the Trailsman' ever since I set foot west of the Mississippi!"

Fargo nodded and let out a little smile. It was always good to be heard of, even if the one who'd done the hearing was on the wrong side of the situation. "Let's get a move on, then. And if you don't mind, I'd like to spend the first chunk of my time in the saddle catching up with my old friend, here, Fred Gant."

Forebush dipped the brim of his hat and smiled wide. "Fine with me, boys!"

They rode on.

Cuchillo Rojo and his people had moved along, all right. By midafternoon, they had arrived at his choice for a new campsite, about ten miles north—give or take—from their former site. He had checked the site well. It was far from any cavalry outposts, and didn't seem to have been visited by whites, either. At least, recently.

The people were starting to erect their teepees and put together a smoke lodge, and some of the women were building a cooking fire where they would roast the many jackrabbits and birds his men had taken along the way. Others were bringing water from the little stream about a half mile to the west. His wife,

Glows Like Sun, was helping Little Feather's woman rope together the ribs of her teepee. How beautiful she was! Every time he looked at her or spoke with her, it was all new. He saw new beauty in her face and form, heard new music in her voice with every encounter.

There would be a feast of celebration tonight, although not like the one there would have been if some brave had taken down an antelope instead of just birds and rabbits. But they were enough.

One made do with what the desert provided, and today it had not provided any big game. But perhaps tomorrow it would. He had seen the fresh tracks of pronghorn as his people entered this sequestered little valley.

Tomorrow he would take what braves could be spared from settling in, and he would go south again, to the rock mountain that stood amid so many sand hills. He could not let the Daughter of Dancing Bird go without protection. He felt bound to her. He hoped that if his son—the son of a white mother, himself—ever came to harm, Daughter of Dancing Bird could protect him in the white world just as Cuchillo Rojo, himself, was protecting her on the desert, the world of the Apache.

"All right, Fred, I think I've got it," Fargo said softly. Although they'd had to be careful about being overheard, they had separated themselves from the rest of the riders well enough that Gant had been able to relay most of his story, and Fargo had been able to put his cards on the table as well.

He'd also been able to relate to Gant to expect a horrific sight as they rode down to the north side of the mountain. Gant swallowed hard, but nodded. Fargo didn't suppose that Gant could be much of a stranger to violence or carnage. Not coming from the background Gant came from, anyway. But he supposed that seeing another result of it was never anything a man looked forward to.

Not a man in his right mind, anyway.

The landscape began to look familiar, and Fargo supposed they couldn't be too awful far from the mountain's north face. When, a few moments later, his nose began to twitch uncomfortably with the scent of bodies left out to rot, he knew it.

He saw Gant mouth, "Dear Lord . . ." before he covered his mouth, and a moment later, Forebush stopped the entire line of men and waved them up to circle him.

One of the men Forebush said he'd found first, a crusty little rascal of a fellow named Whitley, said, "Christ on a friggin' crutch, Forebush! What the hell is that god-awful stench, anyhow?"

Then the men burst a mob of questions and complaints, and it took Forebush a few minutes to get them quiet enough that he could be heard. "Quiet, I said!" he shouted. And when the men were finally still, he said, "Yesterday, I tried to signal the boys up here. I tried to signal for quite a while, in fact. But nobody answered. Nobody even acknowledged seeing the signal. I figured something was wrong, which is why I rolled some of you gents out of the sack in such a rush this morning. And now, with the smell . . ."

"They're all dead, ain't they?" Whitley asked, although it wasn't really a question. "God dammit, Forebush, if you got me up here on those whatchacall, false pretends—"

"Pretenses," muttered Gant.

"—then I'm gonna—"

"Gonna what?" Forebush said. His face was flushed, and there were deep creases sinking furrows into his brow. "Just what are you going to do, Mr. Whitley?"

For once, Whitley kept his mouth closed.

"Good," Forebush said, satisfied. "Now, from the stench of things, I'd say our friends met up with some Apache that didn't cater to them minin' on their land. You follow me so far?"

No one answered, so he went on. "Now, I figure that if they done that yesterday—probably the day before—they ain't hangin' around. They're probably well into Mexico by now. So what we gotta do is go in there and clean up after 'em, and then start breakin' rock."

A couple of groans came from behind Fargo, but it stopped at that because just then, Forebush added, "And they probably left behind a couple or three loads of ore with nobody's name on it, too."

It took not one more word, encouraging or otherwise, to get the men moving again. They filed past Fargo and Gant almost automatically.

Gant didn't comment either way, but Fargo was thinking that maybe, in another circumstance, he'd like to have Forebush on his side.

15

The men rode down into the valley to the south of the mountain a little before sundown, and the sight they found was as bad as its scent had promised it would be. The mutilated bodies of the men, which Fargo had taken care to pile with certain neatness, had been dragged across the camp by scavenging coyotes. A bear had been at the mess, too, and done quite a bit of damage. Fargo was glad they hadn't interrupted him.

Apparently the stench of rotting flesh traveled fast, and the predators that would also scavenge had all arrived as fast as they could. A flock of crows covered the heap of corpses to the east, and a flock of buzzards took the western end. There had been a cougar, Fargo determined, who'd been run off by the bear. Probably a young cat. But he'd still been able to drag off somebody's leg.

As Fargo stepped down off the Ovaro, he said, "Seems a shame to just take all this good meat and throw dirt on it. The native critters are having a festival."

Gant, to whom he'd aimed the remark, suddenly looked a little green and bent to throw up on the weeds. And Gant wasn't the only one. The sound of men upchucking was all around him. It almost gave Fargo the urge to lose his dinner.

But he didn't, and he was one of the men sent in

to check out the tunnels and look for tools. When he came out, bearing seven shovels and five picks, he thought that Forebush was going to try to kiss him.

After dumping the tools, he jumped back and said, "There's more," and quickly took Reckenthaller down the shaft to retrieve the rest.

"You don't remember me, do you?" asked Reckenthaller as they trudged back toward the rear tunnel with its storage closet. "Waco, Texas? 'Bout five years back?"

Suddenly, Fargo slapped his own forehead. " 'Course I remember you! By God! It's Chance Wilson, isn't it?"

Reckenthaller nodded and grinned the boyish grin that Fargo recalled. " 'Cept it's just Reckenthaller now. I'd tell you my first name, but I don't rightly remember it."

Fargo laughed.

"I ain't kiddin' you—I don't. I'm as likely to answer to Alphonse as Cousin Billy these days. Hey, if you get another chance to get close to Gant, ask him if he remembers what first name I told Forebush. Know I told him something."

"Lloyd or Floyd or Puddin' Tame or some such?"

Reckenthaller nodded sadly. Fargo had him remembered as Chance Wilson, boy cattle rustler, and so it was doubly hard for him. But Reckenthaller he was now. Fargo was carving it into his brain when they came to the end of the tunnel and its stone doorway.

"Well, ain't that a trick!" Reckenthaller said when Fargo opened the door, exposing the contents of the closet. He'd left a lantern burning inside on his last trip, so they wasted no time collecting picks and axes and shovels and such.

Reckenthaller shouldered his half. "So, what's the deal, Fargo?" he asked. "This don't seem like the sort of caper you're usually in on."

Fargo knew what he meant. He said, "You come out here with Gant?" When Reckenthaller nodded, Fargo went on, "Then I guess you can figure why I'm here."

For a moment, Reckenthaller's face lit up, reminding Fargo of the boyish good looks presently disguised by his spade beard and mustache, and the thirty pounds or more he had taken off his lanky frame since Fargo last saw him. But his face sobered right away—self-training, Fargo supposed—and he said, "Glad to have you fighting on my side again, Fargo. Been too long."

Fargo nodded just as a shaft of light from the tunnel's entrance came into view. "Feeling's mutual, pal," he said softly. Every sound echoed horribly in the tunnel system.

But instead of responding normally, Reckenthaller horse laughed, then indicated that Fargo should look directly ahead of them. There, of all people, stood Forebush.

"Guess what you told me was right, Fargo," Reckenthaller said between bubbles of laughter. "Mistuh Forebush, suh, Mistuh Fargo was just advising me as to the echoes that can carry throughout these tunnels. You should have seen your face, Mistuh Forebush!"

Even though Fargo and Reckenthaller were a good fifty feet from Forebush, they could both visibly see his body posture relax, and Fargo breathed a sigh of relief. Then Forebush barked out a laugh, as well, and signaled them to him with a wave of his arm.

"C'mon, boys, we've got some buryin' to do."

Sobering immediately, Fargo and Reckenthaller moved along toward Forebush and the tunnel's mouth . . . and the bodies.

"All right, you three start diggin' this trench deeper. Gant, you and Fargo go through the bodies and take any personal stuff off 'em so's I can get it to the relatives. Macy and Reckenthaller, drag those bodies back from where the critters took 'em and pile them on with the rest." Having finished his diatribe, Forebush looked to Reckenthaller, who was standing over a mutilated corpse that was dragged out to the edge of the little clearing. Probably by the bear, by the looks of the tracks.

"What you got there, Reckenthaller?" he asked.

Reckenthaller stood up straight. "A mystery, suh, is most certainly what I have got." He pointed down at the corpse. "This gentleman doesn't seem to have been killed along with the others. I suspect he survived an extra day or so, although I cannot imagine why, judging from the condition of the arm. The arm he pointed to, still intact, was swollen and discolored.

Forebush recognized the telltale signs of a rattler bite right away. He nodded. "That explains who started diggin' this burial trench," he said. "I was wondering about that. He must've survived the Apache only to get tagged by a snake. And then? Hell, I don't know. Maybe the grizzly took him while he was diggin'. The man's a hero any way you care to look at it."

Reckenthaller nodded sagely.

"What you got?" asked a new voice. Fargo.

Forebush again went through his evaluation of the situation, and Fargo shook his head. "Poor bastard," he said, although he was thinking that Forebush had just given a very good excuse for Stubbins' being a little less ripe than the others, and for Fargo's having started digging the grave site. Good thing none of them noticed the bullet hole over Stubbins' heart. He'd been a little concerned about that.

And on top of all that, Forebush had managed to make Stubbins a hero. *Well, all hail Forebush, the maker of myths,* Fargo thought sarcastically.

Aloud, he asked, "Has he got any papers on him?

111

Every hero ought to have a name." And the moment the words left his mouth, he regretted them. What if he had something in there with Fargo's name on it?

But he didn't. He was a poor record keeper, it seemed. All they found in his wallet was a card with his name printed on it—and most of the printing worn off—and the two twenty-dollar gold pieces Fargo had given him for Katie's freedom. It seemed that the old bastard had been tight with his money, too.

A search of what pockets remained on his clothing produced nothing more than a glass marble, a pocket-knife (old and dull), two stove matches, and an old pouch of tobacco.

And that was it.

Forebush took the items, jotted a note with Stubbins' name and his belongings listed on it, and put them in his saddlebag. He looked up. "Let's get on with it, fellas. Daylight's burnin' up fast."

Below, Katie Dugan, who, all day, had been cooped up in the cave her father had blasted for their family home, let her last match burn out and turned to start feeling her way back down the stair steps. When she reached the bottom and let the door swing open, she closed it behind her, then blocked it as Fargo had told her.

He'd also told her to stay down in the little house, but when she'd first heard the faint sounds of men moving overhead, she couldn't help herself from sneaking up to snoop. She was glad she had. She'd heard Fargo's voice, and it was a balm to her spirits.

She went to the kitchen and sat at the table, her head in her hands. If Fargo was back so soon, it meant he hadn't had to go all the way into town. So who was he up there with? It gnawed at her that although she'd recognized his voice and heard another man answer, she couldn't hear well enough to make out any words.

She felt certain that if it was all settled, he would have come to her first. But he hadn't, and the possibilities were eating her up. Who were those men he was with? They couldn't be good, or he would have come to her. They must be thieves—killers, maybe!—or she would have heard from him by now.

But his voice had sounded normal—no, happy—when she heard him speak. Why would an alliance with killers make him glad?

Quickly, she shook her head. No, it was something else, something she didn't understand, and which Fargo was helpless to make her privy to. Perhaps this threw the largest spade of all through her wagon wheel spokes. The unknown was like some gigantic, black, fetid-breathed monster, claws out, teeth bared, backing her into a corner.

Unconsciously, she shivered. And then she sat bolt upright, jerking her chin from her hands, her brow setting with determination. She would not let the monster of the unknown win.

Fargo was back. This was a good thing, wasn't it? Earlier than planned, as well—also good.

She hoped.

Cuchillo Rojo sat under the stars, outside his tent. Inside his wife slept with their four-year-old curled under her arm.

Tomorrow morning he would rally his men and lead them back to the Stone Mountain, where they would do battle, once again, with the White Thieves tormenting the Daughter of Dancing Bird. And then, he had decided, they would come back here and uproot the women and children once again, and travel south, into Sonora, perhaps. The Mexicans were always trailing them, but they were more easily dealt with than the Americans.

These last few years his people had to be moving all the time to avoid both Mexicans and Americans. In years past they had moved a great deal, too, but these pilgrimages had been for more traditional reasons: following game or fresh water sources, or raiding the Hopi or the Yaqui or the Maricopas. Others of his kind raided elsewhere, but he didn't know about the people they raided, other than the Mexicans. They all raided the Mexicans.

He shook his head. The signs told him by the Medicine Man were all good for a fight tomorrow. He told himself that they would take many ponies, as they had the last time. But still, he wished he had never seen Daughter of Dancing Bird's signal and made his vow to keep her safe. He had others to think of.

But he had made the vow, and tomorrow he would carry it out.

He also told himself that this was the last time.

He rose and walked into the teepee. Glows like Sun was indeed sleeping with Sees Silver in her arms. How beautiful she was! He was tempted to wake her and slip quietly between her thighs, as he had so many times before. He loved her. He had given up his other wives so that she could be the most important, the only one. And she had honored him with a son, something his other wives had failed to do.

Tomorrow, after the fighting, he would take her—take all his people—to the relative safety of the south country. And perhaps, for a short time, they could rest.

He sank down on the hides and blankets next to her, so quietly that she did not wake, and closed his eyes. Tomorrow would come soon enough.

*   *   *

Fargo was restless in his bedroll. Everything was done for now: the bodies had been searched, buried, and spoken over; the horses were picketed at the edge of the clearing, where they could get at some grass; Forebush had even sent some of the boys down through the tunnels on a snake-killing mission; and everybody was asleep. Except him.

He had bided his time so far in the hopes of learning something new about what Forebush had planned for the future, but he had decided that he'd have better luck milking granite for whiskey.

At least he had determined which of the boys were on his side. Gant and Reckenthaller, of course. They were officially on the case. And there were two other men, a fair-haired kid of medium height named Macy, and a middle-aged, muscular, bar-brawler of a fellow called Stephens. Fargo was especially glad to learn that Stephens was on their side. He wouldn't have wanted to go up against him in a fight: Stephens looked to him like a fellow who could rip off your arm and then beat you to death with it, if the impulse struck him.

He had called Macy a kid, although he was probably twenty-five or twenty-six. He was of an affable personality, quick to catch on to the other fellows' jokes and always the first to laugh—not only at the expense of others, but at his own. But beneath the jovial outside, there seemed to be a well-muscled force at the core of Macy's makeup.

Fargo wouldn't have wanted to go up against him, either.

He had thought about taking care of the others tonight. Sort of like striking while the iron was hot. But Gant had fallen asleep by the time Fargo figured out where he was sleeping, and Reckenthaller wasn't of a mind to stir up a ruckus tonight.

And so Fargo had gone to bed. And lay there, counting the same stars over and over.

At last, he crawled from his blanket, picked up his rifle, and headed out toward the clearing's edge. He'd heard movement out there, and he didn't figure all those boys wanted to be found asleep by a very large—and very hungry—bear.

16

It was a good hour and a half before he heard the rustling again.

When he located the direction it was coming from, it was still a good bit off—too far for him to see in the moonlight, anyhow—but he could tell that it was big. As quietly as possible, he cocked his rifle and waited.

The stink of the bodies was mostly gone, they having been laid to rest under three or four feet of Arizona clay soil, but if he could still smell it, he imagined it might smell like a ringing dinner bell to a bear. If that was what it was.

Crunch, crunch, crunch.

The animal's footsteps were coming closer and faintly, he heard it grunt. Yes, it was a bear. Great.

Suddenly, the moon was blocked out as it stood up on its two hind feet. It was a Mexican grizzly, one of the bigger ones he'd seen.

And it had seen him.

As the bear roared, Fargo let loose his first shot, directly into the bear's chest. It staggered, but that was all. He pumped another round into the chamber and fired for the head. Another stagger, and then the bear dropped down to all fours in preparation for a charge.

Fargo heard something going on behind him in the camp, but paid it no mind. He was too busy chambering another round and trying to find the bear again through the thick cover of cactus and weeds.

When he saw it, it was heading for him full bore, and he knew this would be his last shot, one way or the other. He aimed at the beast's chest, said a quick prayer, and fired the rifle.

The bear took three more strides—came right up to Fargo's feet, in fact—before it collapsed with a death rattle. And Fargo just sat there on his rock. At this point, bravery had nothing to do with it. He was so shook up that he was frozen into place, and had very nearly shat himself.

Suddenly, cheers rose up from behind him. He slowly turned his head to find the entire camp up and armed, and running his way.

Reckenthaller was the first to reach him. "By God, Fargo!" he said. "If not for you bein' up here, we'd most of us be goners!"

Gant was next. He merely kept repeating, "Mother of God, Mother of God," over and over while he went round and kicked at the bear's corpse, making certain it was all the way dead.

It was.

Man after man came up to shake Fargo's hand or clap him on the shoulder. Two offered to skin the bear and make a nice rug out of him, but Fargo refused. He figured the hide belonged to Katie, although he didn't say so. But he offered the meat to Forebush, even though he doubted the rebels would be alive long enough to eat any of it.

And when he felt his feet were capable of holding him up again, he stood up and inspected his bear. If anyone had asked him, during the charge, how big the bear was, he would have sworn it was fifteen feet standing. Now, seeing it dead, he guessed it was more like eleven and a few inches. No fifteen, but still a big bear.

Gant and Stephens helped him roll it onto its side, and he took out his skinning knife in preparation for the pelting. When he was bent over the bear, his mouth close to Gant's ear, he whispered, "Just exactly when you figure to take these rebs out?"

Gant shrugged.

Annoyed, Fargo hissed, "Now's the time to do it, Fred! Dammit, just get it over with!"

"Get what over with?" asked Whitley, whom Fargo hadn't noticed before.

"Carvin' up this bear," Fargo said quickly. "Gant's takin' the meat for the camp, and I'm takin' the hide." He drove his skinning knife deep into the bear's gut and began to slice upward. "Big one, ain't he?"

Whitley nodded his shaggy head. "Don't believe I've ever seen the like," he said, and walked off quickly lest he be asked to help. Which Fargo had figured he'd do.

He waited until Whitley had joined the other men, back at the dying campfire, then said, "Fred, I'm still waitin' for an answer from you."

Gant paused a moment, then said, "There's a lot of silver to be had for the taking, Fargo."

"There's also a tribe of Apache lurking around here someplace, and in case you haven't noticed, they're mad as hell." When Gant seemed unaffected, Fargo added, "By which I mean that they're madder than usual."

Gant still seemed nonplussed. He shrugged and replied, "I think they caught these boys off guard. We're ahead of the game, because we're kinda halfway expecting them."

"Like you were halfway expectin' the grizzly?"

Gant sighed at that. "That was different. How do we know that it wasn't you, sittin' out here all alone, that brought in this bear?"

"Trust me," said Fargo, who still recalled that delicious bath with the long-waiting Katie, "I don't smell that bad."

Gant ducked his head for a moment. "All right. You made your point. How do you want to handle it?"

Fargo admired the claws on his bear and shuddered again at the idea of them ripping and shredding his flesh. "Depends on you, I guess. You want survivors, or you just want to erase these boys?"

"It's war, Fargo, and they're traitors. As much as I hate to tell you to do it, eradicate them. And may God have mercy upon their souls and ours. When you gonna do it?"

"Tonight," replied Fargo grimly. He wasn't much looking forward to this, either. "I'll wake you."

When he'd finished skinning the bear, Fargo went ahead and cut the best meat from one side of the carcass and piled it inside the pelt. Gant had gone off to bed directly, without slicing any, and Fargo figured part of a side would hold these boys—what few were going to be left, anyway—for a decent amount of time. Surely long enough to take them through the burying and the getting back to town parts.

He piled the meat inside the pelt and dragged it down toward the campfire, slung it to one side, then went over to where the men were sleeping.

Gant was the first one up. Fargo had seen him lie down, and knew he was closest to the fire. While Gant went down to wake Reckenthaller and Macy, Fargo went searching for Stephens.

He found him dozing between Whitley and the other two rebs, and gave him a kick in the boot.

Stephens woke with a start, and for a moment,

Fargo was certain he was going to call out. But he didn't. He gave his head a shake, then slowly and carefully got to his feet. Fargo gave a look down the line. Reckenthaller was already up, and Macy was halfway there.

And just then, there was a loud thud in front of Fargo.

He jumped backward, thinking that Stephens had fallen, but was in midair when he realized that Stephens was down, all right, but he hadn't fallen. There was a young cougar clinging to his back.

Fargo followed his first impulse, which was to shoot the cougar. One shot was all it took—straight through both lungs and the heart—but now everybody had scrambled up. Except for Stephens, who was still trapped beneath the cougar, the back of his head clamped in its jaws and his scalp beginning to rip free.

Other shots were being fired, and a quick glance down the line brought Fargo the image of Reckenthaller gunning down Whitley as he struggled to free himself from his blanket, and of Forebush's back as he ran for the tunnel. Gant aimed his pistol in Fargo's direction, and Fargo was about to shoot back when Gant's slug took down the reb on Stephens' right.

A turn on his heel and a quick fan of his pistol killed the reb who had been sleeping on Stephens' left. However, his gun was drawn and cocked and went off when Fargo's slugs took him. As his body lifelessly fell to the ground, he fired wildly, hitting Fargo in the meat of his right shoulder.

"Aw, hell," Fargo muttered as he turned back around to make certain somebody else wasn't going to put another slug into him.

But he was safe. And it hadn't exactly been the bloodbath he'd been expecting. No, dreading. Forebush was still out there, though. He was likely taking aim from one of those gun ports right now.

121

He waved Gant and Reckenthaller over, sent Reckenthaller to the caves to ferret out Forebush, then dropped to his knees and began to pry at the cougar's jaws. But every attempt to free Stephens from his teeth produced a bloodcurdling scream from the man. Fargo was relieved when Gant dropped down on the other side of Stephens.

"Help me," Fargo said, and together, he and Gant were able to free the massive man on the ground.

They both started, however, at the echoing sound of three shots, coming from the tunnel. Fargo held his breath until it was clear that the figure who emerged was Reckenthaller, dragging Forebush's body behind him.

After breathing a sigh of relief, Fargo sent Reckenthaller to fetch his saddlebags, and Gant to pull three long tail hairs from the Ovaro. When they got back, Stephens was talking, although he wasn't making much sense.

"What's he sayin'?" Reckenthaller asked as he handed over Fargo's saddlebags.

Fargo dug around in one of them until he found a small leather kit, from which he produced a needle and scissors. "He's just tellin' me 'bout a retrievin' dog he used to have," said Fargo, pointing at his head to indicate that Stephens was out of his. "Say, Stephens, tell Reckenthaller what you already told me 'bout that dog of yours."

Reckenthaller was so engrossed in his own disjointed story that he didn't realize that Gant had come up with a fistful of tail hairs.

"I told you three, Gant," hissed Fargo. "Not the whole damn tail!"

"Oh, Daddy didn't believe in dockin' dogs' tails," remarked Stephens. "Said it weren't natural."

"Good for him," Fargo replied, and patted him on

the shoulder. He went back to his saddlebags, and this time pulled out a flask. "Have a drink on me, then keep tellin' about that retrievin' dog."

Reckenthaller took the flask, uncorked it, and held it to Stephens' lips. Stephens took a good sip, but not enough to suit Fargo. "That don't seem fair," Stephens complained when Fargo suggested he take another slug. "You boys ain't had none yet."

Fargo indicated to Reckenthaller, who said, "Don't mind if I do," and pretended to have a drink. "Good stuff, Fargo. Where'd you get it?" He passed the flask to Gant.

While Gant pretended to enjoy the whiskey flask, Fargo threaded one of the stallion's hairs through the needle, then knotted the ends. By the time Stephens was emptying the flask, Fargo had his scalp sewn halfway back on—quite neatly, too, he told himself—and Stephens was recounting the time his daddy had taken both himself and his dog out in search of a schoolhouse's pet skunk named Stinky Stripes McPew, back home in Missouri.

Stephens kept on talking—although with increasing disjointedness—and Fargo kept on stitching, and pretty soon Stephens was all patched up, from his scalp to his back. The attacker's body was that of a young cougar—very thin and scrawny—who looked to be half starved to death, and probably had been desperate.

It would have to have been, Fargo thought, to attack a campful of men.

When he sat back from Stephens, who was now sleeping—and without ever telling them whether Stinky Stripes McPew had ever gotten back to the schoolhouse in one piece—Gant tugged at his sleeve. "And now it's your turn, my friend," he said, and helped Fargo shuck out of his buckskin shirt.

Reckenthaller cleaned and inspected the wound. "Aw, hell," he said. "Just hit the meat. Pour a little whiskey on it, Gant. That'll fix it up fine."

Fargo figured that was easy for Reckenthaller to say. It wasn't him that was shot up. But before he knew what was happening, Gant reappeared with a new flask in hand and forced Fargo to take a long drink, then poured another two capfuls onto Fargo's wound.

It burned like hell, and Fargo gritted his teeth and twisted his head. Before he knew it, Gant had applied a bandage, ordered him to go to sleep, and taken off with Reckenthaller to gather the bodies and prepare them for burial.

It was coming dawn when Fargo woke again. He didn't know how long he'd slept, but it couldn't have been very long, because he was still bone tired. But he figured he'd best rise and shine. The sun was sending pink and purple fingers through the eastern horizon, and the morning breeze was cool.

Gant and Reckenthaller had finished burying the men, and Stephens still lay in the same position Fargo had left him, beneath his blankets. If Fargo felt like crap this morning, he knew it was nothing compared to how bad Stephens was going to feel when he woke.

But he had things to do, and especially a person to see. Katie, waiting below.

He made himself get up and stumbled over to Gant and Reckenthaller, roasting bear meat by the fire.

"Well, mornin'!" Reckenthaller, who saw him first, regaled him. "Hey, Gant, throw another hunk of bear on that fire!"

Turning, Gant saw him, too, and began to search around inside the pelt for another hunk of meat. He found one and had it half threaded on a new spit of mesquite when Fargo held up his hand. "Hold on," he said. "Don't know if I can hold anything down yet." Actually, he knew that he could. Just not bear.

Gant shrugged and shoved the meat back inside the hide. "Your loss," he said with a smile. "Figured to get this hide of yours stretched after breakfast."

"Not today," said Fargo, sitting between them. "We've got to take us a little trip around the mountain, first."

"Why?" asked Reckenthaller. "You got more rebs hid up on the north side, Gant?"

"No, but I've got a Yankee in hiding," replied Fargo.

Both Reckenthaller and Gant said, "What?" at the same time, and Fargo laughed.

"It's not whatever you're thinkin', boys," he said with a chuckle. "My Yank is female, and the rightful owner of this mountain and all the silver in it."

Reckenthaller tossed the stick he'd been playing with into the fire. "Aw, crap," he muttered.

"I don't suppose she'd be averse to giving you boys a small reward, though," Fargo added. "Say, all the ore dug up by the boys before you." He pointed toward two freight wagons parked on the far side of the clearing, both heaped with ore.

Reckenthaller's face lit up again. "Well, say, that'd be grand of her! Like to meet this generous lady!"

"Good enough," said Fargo. Even Gant was looking a tad more chipper. "We'll go after you two have your breakfast."

17

Katie was up with the dawn and pacing a new pathway in the kitchen when she heard something outside. Something not at all like the gunshots she'd heard last night. These were friendly sounds, men's voices. And Fargo's was among them.

When she was sure it was his voice, she began tearing down the barrier she'd erected at the front entrance, her movements becoming more frantic and excited when she realized he was ripping away debris from the other side. "Katie!" he shouted through the small hole. "Brought you some company, honey!"

Suddenly, she stopped moving boards, and her hands went to her hair. And the mule! The whole house smelled of mule!

Torn between excitement and embarrassment, she stood, frozen in place, until Fargo pulled a large board down. She could see his whole face now, and when he saw her he beamed. "You look tastier than fresh apple pie, darlin'," he said, and she laughed and began to tear at her side of the barricade again.

A few more minutes and Fargo and his friends pulled aside the last obstacles, and Katie flew into his arms. "What was the shooting? Fargo, you're hurt! Hello," she said to Gant. "Come in, come in. Fargo, what—"

He kissed her, long and hard, temporarily silencing her. It wasn't what she'd had in mind, but she enjoyed it to the point, when he released her, that she couldn't remember what she was going to ask next.

She stood there, mute and swaying slightly, while Fargo chuckled beside her. "That's my girl. Always knows just the right thing to say. Katie, this is Mr. Gant. Behind him is Mr. Reckenthaller, and Mr. Reckenthaller is pulling Mr. Stephens."

Gant bowed slightly. "It's just Fred, ma'am."

Katie nodded in acknowledgment just before she saw Stephens on the travois Fargo had made for him. Or rather, he had overseen the building of it. She didn't imagine he could do too much with that arm of his.

She squatted beside the travois and gently inspected Stephens' head and back, then looked up at Fargo. "Cougar?" she asked. He nodded in the affirmative and she saw Stephens and Reckenthaller back to her childhood bedroom. She was glad she had taken the time to change the sheets when Stubbins was finally dead.

The one called Fred Gant came in behind them, and helped Reckenthaller put the shirtless Stephens into the bed and roll him onto his stomach.

"My mama always said that air was good for a wound," said Gant, and tipped his hat. Stephens didn't remark one way or the other, being unconscious.

She was busy taking a closer look at the stitches. "Who thought to use horse hair? That was very clever."

"That was Fargo, ma'am," confessed Reckenthaller. "Stitched him up before he'd let anybody look at his own shoulder, too." Chuckling, he shook his head. "That's quite the feller you've got yourself, ma'am."

Unsure of how to reply, she simply nodded. "He has no fever, but I'll pick herbs from out front and make a soothing tea for him. It will help his wounds drain, too."

This time, it was Gant who broke out in a laugh. "What are you, anyway? Part Indian?"

His laughter ceased abruptly when she said, "Yes."

He bowed quickly and muttered, "Sorry, ma'am," fluster coloring his face.

She stood up. "Why? I'm not." She smiled, and left them behind. She had Fargo's wound to look at.

But he wasn't in the house. She found him outside, tending a string of horses, the Ovaro included. And at the end of the line lay a grizzly bear hide!

She walked right past him and knelt beside it, stroking it. "Oh, who has killed this bear? You, my Fargo? Did you kill it? Was that how you got your wound? My mother told me of attacks by the big bears, and how few warriors survived them!"

He grinned and said, "Thought you might like the hide to tan, Katie."

"Oh yes, yes indeed!" she said happily, and then remembered his shoulder. She rose, saying, "And your arm, Fargo? I heard two bursts of shots last night."

He nodded. "The first were for the grizzer. The second for a cougar and some rebs." He paused, grinning again. "We got 'em all. Not before they did us a little damage, though."

She reached to touch his shoulder. "The bear?"

He shook his head. "A reb. Dead one, as a matter of fact. Those Southern folks are gonna be hard to beat."

A quizzical look crossed her pretty face. "A dead man . . . a dead man shot you? I don't—"

"I'll explain the whole thing later, Katie. Right now, I've got these horses to see to, and . . . By the way, how's the mule?"

"Fine."

"Good. I'll put the Ovaro back inside, then. And then I've got a frame to build for the bear's hide."

"I understand," she said, and wandered out into the ruined garden to look for wild herbs for the tea she planned to make for Mr. Stephens. And for her brave Fargo, who she thought should be known, from this day forward, as Bear Killer.

Fargo, now known to at least one person as "Bear Killer," led the Ovaro inside and put him in with the mule. He would have liked to bring the others in, as well, but he didn't know whether they'd choose to eat the bed or ignore it. He'd stretched the hide, though, and leaned it up against the garden fence. Well, what was left of it, anyway.

Katie was out in the kitchen, brewing some tea, he thought, with Reckentaller keeping her company. He wasn't so sure he liked the idea of Reckenthaller being so close to Katie, but there wasn't anything he could do about it without promising more to her than he could give.

Gant was still in with Stephens, he supposed, and he took a peek into the room on his way to the kitchen. Gant was in there, all right, but he'd fallen asleep at the bedside and was using Stephens' feet as a pillow. Poor fellow, Fargo thought. The night had knocked him out. Plus, he didn't imagine that the two-hour trek around the mountain's base had done him any good, either.

Everybody needs sleep, he thought. Even big-time special agents of the U.S. government.

He left the room quietly and went into the parlor and kitchen. Katie greeted him with a big smile. "How's the arm?" she asked.

Actually it hurt like hell, but he said, "It's okay."

"No it ain't, Fargo," said Reckenthaller. "The slug

went clean through, but it chopped up some muscle on its way. You'd best let Miss Katie take a look at it."

Katie lifted her eyebrows and pointed to a chair at the table.

"Oh, hell," grumbled Fargo. "Two against one ain't fair. You know that, don't you?" He pulled out the chair, plopped into it, and began to struggle with his shirt.

Katie stopped his hands with hers. "Let me do it, Fargo," she purred, and he obeyed. Even if he'd been all the way awake, he would have let her do it. He was that tired, and that weak. He didn't know how Reckenthaller was sitting up so straight. He'd been up longer than Fargo had, and by a few hours.

Katie got Fargo's shirt off and he managed not to yelp out loud, and then she made some clucking sounds while she studied his arm. "The same man did not stitch Mr. Stephens." Reckenthaller squirmed in his seat. "This is sloppy work. No wonder it gives you so much pain, Fargo."

Fargo didn't say anything as she rose and pulled a small pot off the stove, but Reckenthaller excused himself and went back to check on Stephens. Or so Fargo assumed. Reckenthaller didn't say.

When Katie returned, she brought the pot and two knives—one sharp and one table—and with the carving knife, carefully cut the stitches from Fargo's wound. A stench rose up, and Fargo made a face.

"You see? If you hadn't come to me in time, you would have lost your arm, if not your life." She shook her head while she bathed the pus away with a damp dish towel. "This wound is right on the edge of going sour. I still may not be able to save the arm."

Fargo made a threatening face, although he didn't really carry it off. "You'd better try your best, Katie girl. That's my shootin' arm you're talkin' about."

"We'll see," she said, and moved to a fresh corner of the dish towel. "We'll just see."

Cuchillo Rojo had started out at dawn, and was now within five miles of the Stone Mountain. Some of the men were still complaining about this raid; others were just as unappreciative of it, but rode in silence. Those who kept their silence were doing themselves a favor, he thought. He would remember the complainers.

The Stone Mountain was in sight now, standing out as it did from the sand hills that surrounded it. It was still a way off, but at least they could see it, and they could focus on it. It gave them something to think about other than why they didn't wish to be here this morning.

He suspected some of them had very good excuses.

He was not one to accept excuses, though, no matter how well thought out or cleverly delivered. Apache had no use for them, not true Apache. You either did something, or you did not. It was that simple, that finite.

Cuchillo Rojo had promised himself that he would do this last thing for Daughter of Dancing Bird. And he would not break his word, not even to himself.

Today he would split his forces before they went around the mountain. That way it would be easier for the men to put themselves in good positions for attacking. The attack itself would be the same as before. Quick, clean, and brutal.

He hoped.

Reckenthaller hadn't woken Gant. He had just left him to sleep sideways on Stephens' bed, and taken a seat across the room, in the corner.

He was so tired, despite the good-looking woman in the other room, that he fell asleep immediately.

He didn't even wake when Katie came in to clean Stephens' wounds.

She saw him sitting in the corner and went to work quietly. She was afraid she would wake Gant, but not afraid of waking Stephens. She wanted to ask him how he felt, although she imagined his answer would be "not so good" or something like that. He was terribly torn up.

He was still lying on his stomach, so all his wounds were in full view. He had suffered a near-scalping by the cougar, but Fargo had taken the time and the effort to reconnect the flesh with an endless series of tiny, careful stitches.

His back and shoulders were messier than the scalp, if possible. The mountain lion had raked Stephens with his hind claws while he hung on with his front, which had left deep, jagged holes in the flesh. The sewing here was not so refined, but it was adequate, she decided. She couldn't see Reckenthaller taking all that time, so the stitcher had to have been either Gant or Fargo.

She cast her vote for Fargo, who, in her opinion, could do no wrong.

She realized, quite suddenly, that she was falling in love. Something she had planned never to do until she was rich, until she had cleaned out this mountain, until she had gone to Europe.

Her shoulders sagging with disappointment, she dipped her rag in the pan of water and began to gently dab at Stephens' wounds.

When she was about halfway through, Stephens suddenly woke with such a start that Katie fell off the bed and Gant sat up straight and blinked at so rudely losing his pillow.

They both cried out, which caused Stephens to echo their cry, which did nothing to wake Reckenthaller, but brought Fargo running.

"Ouch!" repeated Stephens. And then, looking around him, added, "Where the hell are we, anyhow? Just what kind of deal is this?" Then he saw Katie and, wide-eyed, demanded, "Who's she!"

Fargo leaned back against a rocky wall while he caught his breath. "Why don't you ask her friends, out front?"

An odd look crossed Katie's face, and abruptly, she dropped her rags and her pan of water and fairly leapt over the bed. She quickly kissed Fargo on her way to the front hall, leaving the men to blink behind her.

"Who the hell are her friends?" asked a groggy Gant.

"First, somebody tell me where in the devil we are!" demanded Stephens.

Fargo ducked through the doorway and headed for the garden, shouting, "Take it, Gant!"

18

The sight that met Fargo's eyes when he charged outside was one of confusion. Katie was jabbering in Apache to Cuchillo Rojo. Twenty braves or more sat behind him on restless ponies while another half dozen had dismounted and were squabbling over the mounts on Fargo's picket line. Two braves had already come to blows over a blaze-faced chestnut mare, which had been ridden out to the mine by Gant.

"Not the horses!" he shouted before he realized it. He must have moved, too, because the second he became aware that Cuchillo Rojo had pushed past Katie and was making for him, he also became aware of Gant bursting from the tunnel behind him. He shot out his left arm, arresting Gant's progress, and turned to face Cuchillo Rojo.

In Spanish, the warrior demanded, "What goes on here? Why cannot we take the ponies?"

Fargo looked toward Katie, who had the good sense to look a little embarrassed, and asked, "What are they doing here?"

When she didn't answer, but looked at the ground instead, he added, "Smoke signals?"

Katie and Cuchillo Rojo both nodded, Katie still looking at the ground and Cuchillo Rojo with anger, and Fargo knew what had happened. She'd signaled for help, and here it was. Just exactly when they didn't need it.

He turned to face Cuchillo Rojo head-on. "Thank you for coming," he said in Spanish, "but I happened upon some men who helped me to rout the thieves. You may have four horses for your trouble," he added, thinking of the three men he'd fought beside, and the wagons they'd have to haul back to town. They might have to make two trips this way, but he figured that two trips was better than no trips at all.

Gant apparently agreed with him, because there was nothing but silence from his quarter.

Cuchillo Rojo didn't, however. He argued for a while, trying to make the deal better at six ponies, and Fargo finally gave him five. Behind him, Gant started to argue, but Fargo cut him off. He wanted this Apache thing to end agreeably. And hopefully, with everybody alive to talk about it later.

At last, Fargo knew the dickering was over when Cuchillo Rojo pointed at the grizzly hide, stretched to dry and leaning against the high rocks to the west of the cave entrance.

Fargo knew enough Apache to know that Katie proudly touched his arm and said, "He killed it. My brave Fargo. I have given him an Apache name. He is Bear Killer."

In English, Fargo said, "Tell him there's a young cougar pelt for the taking, up around the mountain. He's welcome to it."

She started to relay the information, but Cuchillo Rojo, in Spanish, broke in, "Many thanks to Bear Killer. We will take the cougar pelt. How do we know these men will not come back to hurt Daughter of Dancing Bird or steal from her?"

Fargo said, "These men are friends. When they leave Daughter of Dancing Bird's home, they will be gone forever."

Apparently, this was welcome news to Cuchillo Rojo, who nodded and relayed Fargo's information to his men while Katie translated to English for Gant. She—and Fargo—wanted him very aware that once he and his men were gone, they were gone.

This many braves gathered in the small garden could convince him in a way that Fargo never could, and Fargo knew it.

The Indians took their five horses—including Gant's mount and Reckenthaller's, much to Fargo's dismay—and rode away to the north, when the two braves sent up to get the cougar returned with its pelt. This, in addition to a good supply of bear steaks carved from the remaining grizzly carcass.

They seemed happy with the outcome, as well they should, Fargo thought. It wasn't every day that a man rode a few miles from home empty-handed and returned with fresh meat for the dinner table and fresh horses, as well.

Well, he supposed Apache did that fairly frequently, but this time nobody got killed.

When the Apache had ridden out of sight, Fargo, Katie, and Gant went back inside, leading the remaining three horses in, as well. Katie, who seemed overjoyed with everything, ducked into the kitchen to fetch her herbal tea for Stephens, who was shouting from the back bedroom for somebody to come and tell him what was happening.

Eventually, everybody whose wounds needed tending were tended, whose stomachs required medicine were given it, and whose bellies required food were filled. And an exhausted Katie sat curled beneath Fargo's good arm on the couch. Her lids heavy with exhaustion, she asked Fargo, "Is everything—"

"Done?" he cut in.

"Yes. That," she said.

"Everything but the dishes," said Fargo, but when she stirred, he held her down. "They can wait, Katie. They can wait for a good long while."

She stopped fighting him and began to snuggle closer. "Okay, Bear Killer," she said through smiling lips. "How's the arm?"

"Truth?"

"Of course."

"Hurts like a sonofabitching bastard," he said truthfully.

She shook her head. "You didn't drink the last tea I brought you, did you?"

Quickly, he reached for the coffee table and his neglected mug of the wretched stuff. "Oh, yes, ma'am," he said and took a big gulp. The tea was bitter and tasted of dirt. He made a face and peered at it over the rim.

Katie laughed. "Tree bark. Soon you will start to feel better."

"How come everything that makes you feel better tastes so rotten?"

She laughed softly: a sound like little golden bells. "I can't answer that. The gods' plans, I suppose. They can be playful, you know."

"Some sense of humor," said Fargo, his mouth quirked to one side.

But she touched his hand and pressed the mug toward his mouth. "Drink more. It will work faster."

Fargo breathed a sigh, but he gave in to her demands. Katie was like a force of nature. You had to just shut up and go where she led you.

A half hour later, he was asleep and pain free. And stretched out, smiling, on the parlor sofa.

As the braves rode north, toward the new camp and their women and children, Cuchillo Rojo was still angry. It had not diminished with distance, as he had hoped it would. No, his anger grew with the miles.

He was pleased about the ponies, and pleased about the new cougar pelt, but he was not pleased about having had to roust out his men and ride so far for nothing else. True, he had suffered no casualties, but he had not killed any whites. And secretly, he had been looking forward to killing some whites. And he was not pleased that Fargo, or "Bear Killer" as he was now supposed to think of him, had hidden white men in Daughter of Dancing Bird's home. He would have liked to see them, and how many.

He did not blame Daughter of Dancing Bird. She had been raised in the white world, and knew little of Apache customs and practices. He did blame Dancing Bird, however, for not teaching her daughter the Apache way.

But Dancing Bird was dead. He could not censure her now.

Juanito, his second in command, rode up to ride beside him.

"We got the best of their ponies," Juanito said in Apache, expecting some sound of agreement from Cuchillo Rojo. He received none, and was puzzled. "What is it?" he asked. "Should we have taken the black instead of the roan?"

Cuchillo Rojo shook his head. "No. You chose wisely. The horses are fine."

"I am puzzled, then."

Cuchillo Rojo turned toward him. "We killed no whites. When we ride out to kill whites, I expect to do just that. Kill white men."

Juanito scowled. "Someone did. There were many graves when Talking Owl and I rode to get the cougar pelt and the bear meat. Tonight the women will roast the bear, and we will have a feast. The other men are glad they didn't have to fight for their dinner, Cuchillo Rojo."

This soothed Cuchillo Rojo somewhat, but he was still not pleased. And it showed on his face.

Juanito said, "I am certain we will run across other whites on our journey south, Cuchillo Rojo. We can have a good fight with them, instead, and maybe take more ponies."

Cuchillo Rojo's face softened slightly. "True."

"Perhaps these new whites will have whiskey."

Cuchillo Rojo's expression softened further. "Perhaps they will. I hope they will."

The promise of whiskey, even imagined whiskey, went a long way with Cuchillo Rojo. Even if he had killed today, he would have counted no whiskey among the spoils. He had asked Daughter of Dancing Bird, and she had told him they had none. He had seen Fargo, too. He was badly wounded in the arm, perhaps in the fight with the other whites, perhaps when he killed the bear. If they had had whiskey, Fargo would have been drinking it, and he'd seen no signs of whiskey in his words or actions.

"Thank you, Juanito," he said after a moment. And then, as an afterthought, he said, "You will take the cougar pelt. I have no use for it."

Juanito came as close to a grin as he was capable. "Thank you, Cuchillo Rojo. My woman will be happy to have a new hide to tan."

Cuchillo Rojo had many pelts and hides, and although a cougar pelt taken in a raid was a good coup, he would rather let Juanito take it. He said nothing, but he would take the chestnut mare they had brought along. She was very nice, and bred to his pinto stallion, would produce fine, tall, young colts and fillies.

He wished they had taken Fargo's stallion, though. A Medicine Hat paint was always good luck.

"Let us pick up the pace, then," he said to Juanito. "Your woman waits for her cougar hide!"

139

With that, he gave the signal, and the entire line of warriors kicked their ponies into a lope. Things were better, now that he had talked with Juanito. He was not so angry anymore, and there would be no need to go back and kill a few whites.

There would be other whites, and perhaps they would have whiskey.

19

Although Stephens was healing, his pain did not lessen. By the next morning it seemed to grow worse, and Katie was worried. She confided in Fargo that she had made his tea double strength that morning, but it seemed to have no effect.

"Don't worry so, Katie," Fargo said to soothe her.

It didn't work. "I cannot help it," she said. "He is very badly injured. Perhaps he should go to town and see a white man's doctor, but I don't know that he is strong enough to make the journey, even with Erasmus pulling him."

"Erasmus?"

"I named the mule. He has been too long without one."

"Katie, trust me. When Stephens comes back into himself, he'll be strong enough to pick up Erasmus and throw him to town from here. He's just healing—that's all." He doubted she'd ever seen a man really seriously injured in her short life. Of course, Stephens looked like he'd been poleaxed, but not any worse than he should. In fact, Fargo thought both he and Stephens were healing up pretty damned fast, all things considered, and he told her so.

She made a face at him. "You, yes. You are healing

like magic was spun all around you. But not Stephens."

"He's just healin' like a normal human being, girl. Now, stop fretting. There's something else I want to talk to you about."

She leaned toward him and propped her head in her hands. "Go on. I'm listening."

"Katie, I've been thinkin' that I'm gonna have to be movin' on here pretty soon, and I think you should—"

"What?" she said, sitting up in a rush. "Where is it you have to go that I can't go with you? And why do you think I'd let you?"

" 'And why do you think I'd *let* you?' " Fargo repeated angrily. "You'd *let me*?"

Katie sat back, her brows working. It was obvious that she knew she'd gone too far but wasn't sure why. She didn't say a word.

Finally, an irritated but still gentle Fargo said, "Look, Katie, that's why I have to leave, don't you see? I've never let anybody run my life, and never will. I care about you, Katie, but not enough to hand my life over to you."

Still she sat there, looking not at him now, but at the tabletop. Quietly, she said, "That is what falling in love is? Handing over your life? Handing over your furniture?"

He nodded.

Her head dropped farther. "Then I have fallen in love," she said softly. "I'm sorry, Fargo. I didn't mean to. . . . I'm sorry."

She was obviously hurt and flustered, and he scooted back his chair and held out his arms. "Come here, girl."

Suddenly she was in his lap and bawling her heart out and making him feel like he deserved a good, swift kick in the britches, if only he could figure out how to do it.

There was a rustle in the hall doorway. Fargo

looked up and saw Reckenthaller. "Um . . . I ain't botherin' you folks any, am I?"

Fargo's "Oh, no, not at all," delivered in what he'd thought was a very sarcastic tone, did nothing to dissuade Reckenthaller. He stepped into the room, hat in his hands, and walked up to Fargo's chair.

"What is it?" Fargo asked when Reckenthaller failed to further the conversation.

"Me and Gant been talkin'," Reckenthaller said while Katie, whom he had yet to recognize, sobbed silently in Fargo's arms. "Talkin' about what to do about the ore and such. And Stephens. You know."

"I'm at a loss."

"You know, talkin' about how to handle stuff. Gettin' back to Tucson, for one thing."

Fargo's brain clicked. He said, "Tell you what. Why don't you two go ahead and take what ore you can into town? Leave Stephens here. We'll take care of him until you get back. All right?"

"Can we borrow your mule?"

"Isn't that what you were tryin' to ask in the first place?"

Reckenthaller shuffled his feet. "Well, sorta."

Fargo readjusted Katie on his lap. "Yes, take the mule. Just don't lose him in a card game in town. And come back soon as you can. I've got to be moving on myself, pretty soon."

Katie began to sob harder even as Reckenthaller said, "You do? Where you headed?"

"Don't know yet. Might follow the sun and head on out toward California. Might go on back east for a bit, maybe as far as Texas." He kept his destination as vague as possible, which was easy since he didn't really have one in mind, yet. He didn't want Reckenthaller offering to tag along, even if he did like the kid.

"Well, don't just stand there," he finally added. "It's already past nine. Get goin'!"

"Oh. Sure. Well, see you, Fargo," Reckenthaller added before he turned around and started for the hall.

"Hey, Reckenthaller?" Fargo called.

"What?"

"The one of you that's not leading the horses up there can take a shortcut up through the mountain, okay?"

"Tell Gant," Reckenthaller said, and disappeared into the front hall.

"You're going so soon?" asked a small, muffled voice, and then Katie lifted her head. "Tomorrow or the next day?"

Fargo said, "Yes, Katie. That soon."

"You will leave me, even though you know how I feel about you?"

Although he didn't really know how Katie felt about him, he was inclined to believe that she didn't, either. She was just a little sweet on him. After all, she hadn't had a grown-up relationship—or really, a nonbrutal one—with a man before. He was her first love. But there would be others. And he told her so.

At which, she began crying again.

"Katie, stop it," he said as kindly as he could. "You're a beautiful woman. You can have your choice of men."

"But it's you I want!" she cried.

"No, you don't. You just think that now. Why, right now, you could have Reckenthaller if you wanted him."

Her head came up and a quizzical expression overtook her. "Reckenthaller?" Obviously, she'd never even thought of the possibility.

"You don't see the way he looks at you?"

She shook her head, giving him a shrinking feeling. He pulled her up so that she had to look him in the eye. "Katie, you and I are going to have to have a long talk about men and the world, all right?"

"All right," she said softly.

"Now for the quiz," Fargo said. It was late in the afternoon, not too long before sunset would come. Gant had been shown the secret staircase, and had left to join Reckenthaller hours ago. Stephens was sleeping soundly in Katie's old bedroom—this time without Gant hugging his legs.

Katie asked him if she needed a pencil and paper, and he laughed. "Not that kind of test, Katie. And anyway, I thought you'd never been to a school!"

She tilted her head to one side. "I've heard stories," she said cryptically.

He laughed and she smiled with him, only the second smile he'd seen from her the whole day. Admittedly, it hadn't been a day for a great deal of smiles. He had gone through a series of what symptoms he knew so she could tell if a man had the clap. And that she shouldn't sleep with him then, no matter how great the urge.

He'd told her a number of "lines" men used on saloon girls (and, he suspected, on regular girls, too) and to avoid those fellows. That whiskey was bad for Indians and that she should avoid it at all costs.

He figured that her mother would have told her about pregnancy, and he was glad to avoid the issue. He sure wasn't any expert on how to raise a baby, or what women went through when they were pregnant. All he knew was that half the time those babies were boys and the other half they were girls. If they were boys, chances were that sooner or later he'd face off with them. And if they were girls, well . . .

But he wasn't going to quiz her on any of those subjects, nor on several others he'd had to bring up,

145

like how to open a savings account at the bank and where to take her ore to sell it, or things she needed to buy at the mercantile in town—foods she couldn't grow here and cloth and sewing supplies and ammunition. Instead, he was going to stick to the basics. Which were how to protect herself when she was on her own.

He said, "First, should a young lady sleep with a young gentleman when they first go walking?"

"Absolutely not," she answered, immediately grasping his playful take on the subject at hand. "That would show that she's badly bred. And of course, that he was, too. But then, young gentlemen are held to a much lower standard than young ladies."

Fargo nodded sagely. "I think you've captured the essence of the entire thing, my dear. Whenever he urges you to say yes, you say no. Easy as pie."

She frowned. "I don't like these rules, Fargo."

"You don't have to like them, honey," he replied. "Just live by them. If you want to be greeted well by good society, that is, let alone high society."

She sniffed. "All right."

"Good girl. Now, a gentleman forcing himself on a woman. Is that a good thing or a bad thing?"

She made a face. "Bad."

He nodded. "And what should a lady do if a man tries to force himself on her?"

She giggled. "Shoot his balls off."

"Well, something on that order, I think, although maybe not quite so severe. Use your judgment."

She nodded.

"Now, what about the Apache?"

She sighed. "I'm not supposed to send smoke signals again, because that would let someone know I'm here."

"And?"

"And nobody should know I'm here alone, because

they might try to take advantage of me. Like the other men Stubbins sold me to, or maybe even worse."

"And what should you do if you have trouble?"

"I should follow the south trail over the Santa Ritas and go to the sheriff in Tucson. And follow my instincts. And use my judgment."

"Correct!" said Fargo proudly. "By the way, Katie, where'd you sleep last night? You weren't with me on the sofa or back in your room with the other men."

"In the bathtub," she said, smiling, then looking past him, toward the front hall. "I believe it has gone dark outside."

"I believe you're right," Fargo said, and went to throw a couple of doors across it, to block it from the outside.

He came back to find Katie making a bed on the floor. A bed for two, he noted, not one. Hadn't she been listening to anything he said? Hadn't she understood that she wasn't supposed to sleep with men anymore, even him?

"What the hell are you doing?" he asked her.

When she turned to look up at him, she was smiling, which was not at all what he had expected. He thought that as he blinked in surprise.

She winked at him and said, "Fargo, I am only following my instincts."

20

She made his bed and ordered him into it while she went to check on Stephens. And when she came back, she was nude.

He had never seen her like this before. In the short period of time that they had been making love, she had always been partially covered by pelts or a dress or a blanket, or hidden in darkness. But not tonight. Tonight she came to him bathed only by the light of two candles she'd left burning, and he couldn't have imagined how lovely she was.

He knew her breasts were high and round, but not so perfectly formed as they really were. The skin that covered them was taut and without blemish, and her nipples were large, tight with desire, and the color of salmon when it's broiled.

Beneath the blanket, he felt himself already stiffening.

She took another step toward him. He held up a hand, though, and said, "Stop, Katie. I want to look at you."

She stopped and let him look.

Her waist was tiny, tinier than her clothing ever let on, and belled softly into lean, muscular hips that tapered into long, strong but delicate legs. At their juncture was her mound of Venus, a dark triangle of thick, black hair.

He said, "Turn around," but she had something else in mind.

"Only after you pull down that blanket, Fargo," she said. "You're not the only one who wants to have a good look."

He acceded to her demand, and she looked at him a good, long time before she finally turned her back toward him. He admired the small of her back and the round, high globes of her buttocks for a few moments before he asked, "Did you like what you saw?" Her hair cascaded down her back in long, black waves.

"May I turn again?"

"Yes," he said, wondering why she hadn't answered.

She faced him once more, but this time she held out her arm and pointed at him. "Can I touch it?"

His erection, which had been in danger of going away, suddenly stiffened. "Be my guest," he said, smiling.

She came to him and knelt, and took him into her hands. She had a gentle touch, and a natural way about her, and it. "Is it always so hard?" she asked.

He almost laughed out loud, but held it in. He said, "Only when it's around such great and willing beauty as yours, Katie Dugan."

She played with his shaft for a little while, stroking it, cuddling it, then asked, "May I kiss it?"

"If you want," he said, barely hiding his eagerness.

She did, her lips barely skimming the head, and when he couldn't help but groan her name, she kissed it again and again, then opened her mouth and took half of him into it. She began to lave him with her tongue, then suckle him like a foal at his mama's teat bag.

Soon, Fargo was barely capable of speech. He

clutched handfuls of the blankets and squirmed and tried to tell her to stop, to wait, to hold on, to just . . .

He came with a sharp, tremendously hard spasm that shivered through his whole body, twisting his limbs and contorting his face. He felt his hips buck and knock her aside, and then he fell back on the blankets, limp and exhausted.

He felt her hands on his stomach, then his chest as she slid up his body. He heard her ask, "Fargo, are you all right? Did I do it wrong?"

"Oh, everything was so right," he muttered as he slowly enveloped her in his arms. Even his bad arm was good tonight.

She hugged his body with hers and whispered worriedly, "Did I break it? It's getting smaller all the time!"

He laughed a little, couldn't help it, but when she punched him in the chest, he said, "I'm fine, Katie. I just need a little time—that's all."

"Time?"

He rolled slightly to kiss her on the forehead. "What you see now is how it is most of the time. Small. Easy to tuck away."

"Why was it so big and hard before?"

"Because that's how a man gets when he's sexually excited by a woman."

"But—"

"Katie?" he said, cutting off what promised to be a whole string of increasingly harder-to-answer questions. "Hush up and kiss me."

"But wait—I think I—"

He covered her mouth with his.

Fargo had told her much during the day. But she liked what he was teaching her now even better.

His hands floated up and down her back, her sides, her hips, her backside, then cupped her breasts, holding them captive while each waited for a turn with his mouth. She loved the way he teased her with his teeth and his tongue and his lips, almost hurting her but not really, his touch making her more and more . . . what was it that he'd said? Ah, yes, sexually excited.

Sometimes he made her so excited that she wanted to . . . She didn't know what she wanted to do, but whatever it was, she wanted to—no, needed it—in a big hurry. And now he was doing it to her again.

She felt him slip his hand between her legs, touching her inside, and she moaned out loud, calling his name as if beseeching a god. His fingers began to move on her, within her, stirring her to new heights. She pressed her hips against his hand, trying to get so close to it that they became one, that she could always have this feeling.

But he pulled away, then rolled her atop him, her legs splayed. He kissed her deeply, and while she returned it, he took her hand in his and moved it between their bodies until it met the hardness of his shaft, now again fully erect.

She needed no more prompting. She inched her way back until she felt him pressing at her threshold, silently demanding entrance. Which she willingly granted with a backward thrust of her hips.

They both gasped at the suddenness of it, and she lay still for a second until she had the presence of mind to sit up, to bring her legs forward so that her knees gripped the sides of his chest.

"Yes, Katie, yes, perfect," Fargo groaned. He reached forward, running his hands up her thighs and back again, over and over. She felt him within her, throbbing, twitching, hard and demanding. Without thinking, she began to ride him—slowly at first, then with increasing intensity—and found she could make his manhood go where she wanted. She experimented with the situation, watched and learned as his eyes grew wider and her own pleasure deepened.

And deepened.

And deepened.

Until she found a place that was so intense, so sweet, a tiny movement so deliciously marvelous, that she kept riding, and kept riding until her eyes were closed. And Fargo's fingers tugging at her nipples were like fire, a fire than ran down through her belly to the core of her womanhood on a fine, silver thread. And then the fire engulfed her.

She felt Fargo bucking beneath her, between her legs, felt him spasm right along with her, then melt with her as she collapsed on the furry pelt of his chest.

Late that night, Stephens awoke. Katie heard him call out, and she rose, threw a blanket around herself, and went to his room, carrying a candle.

"Mr. Stephens?" she said softly from his doorway. "Mr. Stephens, did you call? Are you all right?"

He gestured to her to come closer, and she did, bending down toward his face. He was still on his stomach, and the wounds on his back and scalp looked much better than they had earlier in the evening.

"Yes," she heard him whisper. Then, "Who are you?"

"My name is Katie Dugan," she said in reply. "I have been nursing you."

"Thank you, ma'am," he said, and tried to roll over. But he groaned with the effort, and she helped him get back flat on his stomach on the mattress while he thanked her again.

"It is no trouble," she said. "You must lie still and let your wounds heal, all right?"

He nodded and said, "What happened to me?"

"A cougar attacked you. Fargo saved your life and brought you to me."

"A cougar?"

"Yes. The Apache came this morning and took the

pelt." She was pleased to hear him speaking. She didn't know what the others had told him, or if he remembered it, so she kept her voice calm and low, and answered his questions simply but truthfully.

He seemed a little confused, but his fever had broken, much to her happiness. She asked him, "Are you hungry? I can fix you something to eat."

"If it wouldn't be too much trouble, ma'am."

She nodded. "No trouble at all. Just wait here and lie still, all right?"

"Thanks," he said, his eyes fluttering closed again.

She went back to the kitchen, passing a satiated Fargo along the way. She smiled at him. How wonderful he was! She had taken him at his word this afternoon. He was going, and that was the way it was. There was nothing she could do to change it. But she still felt a tinge of sadness, particularly after their fervid lovemaking earlier in the night. Would she find another man to make her feel the way he did?

She pulled a coffee can, stolen from upstairs by Fargo, down from the cupboard and measured out enough to make a partial pot. After she set that on to boil, she took down the plate with the leftover bear steak from her and Fargo's dinner, and began to slice it into manageable pieces.

A few moments later, she had fixed a tray with meat, fried potatoes fixed the way Fargo liked, and hot coffee. She carried it in to Stephens, who was very grateful, and ate every last scrap before nodding off again.

21

The next morning found Reckenthaller and Gant in Tucson. They had driven in last night after dark and slept at the livery atop the two loads of ore they'd been able to bring in. The horses and Katie's mule dozed gratefully in stalls deep in straw, before mangers filled with fresh alfalfa hay. For them, the mule especially, this was like a holiday.

The hostler, Tracy Deeds, came in just as the sun was breaking the horizon. Finding strangers camped in his stable was nothing new to him. Usually they were miners or pilgrims who had pulled into town too late to find anything open. These fellers must be miners, he thought, judging from the ore wagons they were stretched out on.

He recognized Gant after a moment. He'd been in with that bunch who'd rented the horses the other day. He patted Daisy, one of those horses, on her flank as he passed her stall. She looked fit enough, and he nodded in appreciation.

He stopped beside the first wagon and rapped on its side. "Mr. Gant? Mr. Gant, it's mornin'."

Gant roused, shaking his head.

"Good mornin', Mr. Gant," Tracy said. "I see you made it back."

Gant stretched his back and sat up. "Yes," he said. "Sorry. I'm sore."

"Don't doubt it. A bed o' rocks ain't the best for slumberin'." Tracy scratched at his chin, wondering how to ask Gant where the other stable horses were. Also, the other men. It could be rough out there.

Gant rubbed his own neck. "I'll quote you on that, if I may."

Tracy shrugged. "You may, I reckon. I was just wonderin', I mean, you left with more men an' horses than this."

Gant nodded. "Apache. Stole most of the horses, killed most of my men." He fumbled at his pocket. "I can pay you for the horses."

"Apache? This far north? You'd best talk to the sheriff 'bout that. He'd want to know."

"Yes. Yes, we will, as soon as we get this ore delivered and get back out there to pick up the last survivor."

Tracy decided not to press him any further, but he collected money for four horses and accepted an IOU for the other one.

Gant woke his friend, and they set out for Cordy's Place to grab some breakfast, leaving Tracy to guard the ore carts and hitch up their teams. They said they'd drop the ore at Carson's on their way out of town and would see him again in a day or two.

He watched them walking to Cordy's, shaking his head. Eight had ridden out, and only two had been back this morning. Now, they said they'd left somebody behind, somebody who was hurt, but the odds were pretty lousy out there. He turned back toward the livery and started for the first stall. He was just glad his papa had bought the livery before he died.

He saw the Thompson kid, young George, walking down the street, and flagged him down. "Hey, George, you wanna send the sheriff over my way soon's you can?"

George waved, then took off at a lope. It wouldn't be long. He led the mule from its stall and began to hitch it up.

You wouldn't find Tracy Deeds out there in the middle of all those savages and thieves, grubbing for bright metal, no sir. He'd just rent horses and take care of livestock and sell tack to those who wanted to chance it.

He liked living too much to take a chance.

When Gant and Reckenthaller returned from breakfast, they found Sheriff Tyler waiting for them. He asked far too many questions to suit Gant's patience, but finally let them leave on the promise they'd come to his office when they got back to town.

Gant was annoyed, but didn't show it in front of the constabulary. He wasn't dumb, just short on time.

He and Reckenthaller had to drop off this ore, stop by the telegrapher's office, and get on their way if they wanted to be back by sundown.

Which they did.

When at last they had traveled the distance—which the horses and mule made in several hours less time, not being burdened with the ore on this trip—they decided to leave the wagons on the south side of the mountain, and take the horses and the mule on back around to the north.

When they finally rode up to the cave, it was open and Katie was outside, washing laundry. She waved at them and called Fargo outside, then grabbed the mule's lead rope and took him back inside the tunnel.

She was sensational, Reckenthaller thought as he watched her walk away. What a waste of woman-flesh, her out here mining for silver when she ought to be in town, up on the stage or something. He shook his head. What did he know, anyhow? He didn't have two nickels to rub together.

He was pleasantly surprised—and so was Gant—when Stephens hobbled out of the cave behind Fargo. He was healing nicely, although Reckenthaller didn't believe Stephens would ever have his hair cut real short again. Too many scars near the scalp line.

Over dinner, Gant revealed his plans to take the last wagonful of ore back to Tucson, then go wherever his new orders sent him. Reckenthaller himself was thinking about quitting. He liked Tucson, and he liked Katie even better.

This plan seemed the better of the two to him, especially when Fargo announced he was heading out tomorrow, too, but Reckenthaller wanted to talk to Katie alone before he did anything rash. If only he could figure out how to talk to her without sticking his foot in his mouth . . .

He knew that Gant wouldn't mind him quitting. He had another good man in Stephens. That had been discussed over dinner, too, and Stephens seemed willing.

In the end, Fargo bedded with them in the little bedroom at the back, leaving the parlor for Katie and easing Reckenthaller's mind greatly. And he got to talk to Katie alone, outside by the pump stand.

He'd come back, there was no doubt. Fargo was out of the picture, according to her. And she'd need somebody to help with the heavy lifting part of digging for bright metal. He was coming back as hired help, but he figured it wouldn't be too long before things changed for the better.

Before his life, and hers, changed forever.

Fargo lay awake long after everyone else had gone to sleep, thinking about Katie. Thinking about leaving

Katie. And feeling rotten about what he was doing to her.

Oh, he was sure she'd be all right, certain she'd get along and have a place to sleep and food to eat and be protected—he had not one doubt in his head that she'd be back on those smoke signals at the first signs of serious trouble, no matter what she'd promised him.

And he also had no doubt that she'd make a go of this mining operation. If anybody could stick it out, it was Katie.

In the dark, he smiled and shook his head. Yes, his Miss Katie Dugan would miss him for a while—just like he was going to miss her—but in the end, she'd be as fine as frog's hair.

Over on the bed, he heard Reckenthaller toss in his sleep and grumble out, "Yes, Miss Katie . . ."

She'd be fine, all right.

Better than fine.

Idaho, 1860—the trail to hell just got worse.

The ten canvas-topped turtles rattled and creaked as
they wound into the mountains at the lumbering rate
of fifteen miles a day. On good days. On days when the
going was steep or the weather was bad or one of the
wagons broke down, they lumbered less.

The tall rider in buckskins had no trouble keeping
them in sight. He was broad of shoulder and slender
of hip, with pantherish muscles that rippled when he
moved. His white hat, brown with dust, was worn with
the brim low over his eyes to shield them from the
harsh glare of the relentless summer sun.

His name was Skye Fargo. He wore a Colt and had

a Henry rifle in his saddle scabbard and a double-edged Arkansas toothpick in an ankle sheath, and he knew how to use all three with uncommon skill. As a tracker, he was without peer. He also possessed an uncanny memory for landmarks and a superb sense of direction. A lot of folks got lost in the wilds; Fargo never did. A lot of folks couldn't tell east from west or north from south, but Fargo always knew. He relied on the sun and the stars and his own inherent senses, and they never failed him.

Quite often, Fargo used his skills scouting for the army. At other times he hired out for whoever struck his interest. At the moment he was shadowing the wagon train to earn the one thousand dollars he was being paid to find out what had happened to a missing family. A thousand dollars was a lot of money at a time when most men barely earned five hundred a year. Not that Fargo would hold on to it. With his fondness for whiskey, cards, and women—not necessarily in that order—he spent every dollar he made almost as soon as he made it. A friend of Fargo's once joked that his poke must have a bottomless hole, and the joke wasn't far from the truth.

So here Fargo was, astride his Ovaro a quarter mile to the east of the wagons, riding at a leisurely pace and wishing he was in a cool saloon somewhere with a willing dove on his lap, a bottle of red-eye at his elbow, and a full house in his hand.

Fargo had been trailing the wagon train for over a week now. The wagons were filled with settlers, and Fargo wasn't all that partial to their kind. There were too damned many, swarming from the east like locusts, fit to overrun the west with their farms and their cattle and their caterwauling children. As yet only a few areas west of the Mississippi River had become civilized, but give them fifty years and Fargo worried that the untamed prairies and mountains he loved so much would become an unending vista of settlements, towns, and cities.

Fargo dreaded that day. City life was all right for a festive lark, but too much of it bored him. Worse, after a couple of weeks of having a roof over his head and being hemmed by four walls, he got to feeling as if he were in a cage. He couldn't stand that feeling.

The Ovaro pricked its ears and looked toward the wagons, prompting Fargo to do the same. "Damn," he said, annoyed with himself. He hadn't been paying attention, and two riders had left the wagons and were coming directly toward him. For a few tense moments he thought that they'd spotted him. But that was unlikely. He was far enough back in the trees that he blended into the shadows.

Fargo didn't want to be seen until he was ready. Reining toward a cluster of boulders, some as big as the covered wagons, he swung behind them and dismounted. Palming his Colt, he edged to where he could see the riders approach.

The pair were scruffy specimens. Their clothes had never been washed and their hats were stained, their boots badly scuffed. The rider on the left was short and stout, with a face remarkably like a hog's. The rider on the right was big and wide and wore a perpetual scowl on a scarred face only a mother could love. They slowed as they neared the woods and shucked rifles from their scabbards.

Hunting for game, Fargo reckoned. He strained to hear what they were saying, but they weren't close enough yet. He was concerned they would see the Ovaro's tracks, but they entered the trees at a point a dozen yards north of him.

The pair were prattling away, seemingly without a care in the world.

The hoggish one gave voice to a high-pitched titter more fitting for a saloon girl.

"Ain't it the truth, Slag. Ain't it the truth. I don't know how that dirt grubber puts up with it."

"He does it for the same reason any man does," Slag said in a voice that rasped like a file on metal.

"I'd as soon slit my throat as be nagged and badgered and insulted to death."

"You don't have to worry, Perkins. Neither one of us will ever hitch ourselves to a dress."

Slag drew rein and his companion did the same. Both shifted in their saddles and gazed back at the plodding wagons. "Look at them. Like so many sheep. Makes me glad I'm a wolf."

The two men laughed.

"I can't wait to get there," Perkins said. "For me, the best part will be the carving."

Slag snorted. "I believe it. Don't take this wrong, pard, but you're twisted inside. To watch you gives me the chills."

"Why, that's just about the nicest thing anyone's ever said to me," Perkins gleefully responded.

"It wasn't meant to be. You're spooky, is what you are. You should have been born a redskin. You would fit right in as an Apache or one of those devil Sioux." Slag paused. "Now there's something I never thought I'd say to a white man."

Perkins lost some of his good mood. "You make me out to be worse than I am. And you like to carve, too. You're just not as honest about it as I am."

"The hell I'm not. I don't brag about it, is all. Or wallow in the blood, like you do."

Excerpt from *IDAHO GOLD FEVER*

"There are a few with this bunch who could stand to be cut. Take that Rachel."

"Her? She's as sweet as can be."

"I like the sweet ones best."

"I'm glad I'm not sweet," Slag said.

Perkins cackled uproariously.

Lifting their reins, the pair rode on. Soon the vegetation swallowed them and the clomp of hooves faded.

Fargo stayed where he was. He had heard enough to quicken his suspicions. The question now was what to do about it? He wasn't a lawman. He could go for one but it could take weeks to find a federal marshal and bring him back, and by then whatever Slag and Perkins and their friends were up to would be done with.

Twirling his Colt into its holster, Fargo forked leather. He had a decision to make. The people with the wagon train were nothing to him. He didn't know any of them personally. And given his low opinion of settlers, he should rein around and leave. But there were women and children. And there might be a link between this bunch and the missing family.

With a sigh, Fargo reined toward the wagon train. Once he was in the open, he rode parallel with the wagons but stayed a good hundred yards out. Soon shouts told him he had been spotted. Before long several riders came galloping toward him. One yelled for him to stop.

Fargo drew rein and waited.

Two of the three were settlers. Their homespun clothes and floppy hats marked them as members of the wagon train.

The third man was different. He was like Slag and Perkins; dirty and ill-kempt and bristling with weapons. Of middling height, he favored a Remington revolver worn butt forward on his left hip. He had high cheekbones and beady eyes and a hooked nose that made him look like a hawk.

"We want to talk to you, mister," the hawk-faced man declared.

"You see me sitting here," Fargo said as they came to stop. "What do you want?"

The settlers smiled in friendly greeting but the hawk-faced man placed his hand on the butt of his Remington.

"I don't much like your tone."

"I don't much care," Fargo informed him. "Unless you have something to say, I'll be on my way."

"We want to know who you are and what you're doing here."

Fargo shook his head.

"You won't say?" one of the settlers asked.

"My personal affairs are my own."

"What if I insist?" the hawk-faced man said, and just like that his gun hand moved.

So did Fargo's. In the blink of an eye he had his Colt up and out. All three of them heard the click of the hammer. "Draw that six-shooter and I'll blow you to hell."

Amazement turned the hawk-faced man to stone. He stared into the barrel of the Colt and his Adam's apple bobbed up and down. "That was mighty slick."

"Get your hand off that hog-leg."

Reluctantly, the hawk-faced man splayed his fingers and held his arm out from his side. "I meant what I said. That was about the slickest I've ever come across."

The biggest settler, who looked to be in his forties and packed a lot of beef on his bones, kneed his sorrel closer. "Enough of this, Mr. Rinson. I won't have you threatening everyone we come across." He grinned at Fargo. "Forgive him, mister. He means well. He just wants to protect us and our families."

"Is that what he's doing?"

The big settler nodded. "He works for Victor Gore. Maybe you've heard of him? He used to be a trapper in these parts. Or so he tells us."

"Never heard of him," Fargo admitted. But that wasn't unusual. The height of the trapping trade had been before his time.

"Well, be that as it may, Mr. Rinson works for Mr. Gore. We've hired them to guide us to the Payette River Valley. We're farmers, you see, and Mr. Gore says the valley is perfect for homesteading." The man offered his big hand. "I'm Lester Winston, by the way. My family is in the first wagon yonder. In the other wagons are friends of ours. We're all from Ohio."

Fargo slid the Colt into its holster, then shook. Predictably, the farmer had a grip of iron.

"I take it you have heard that the Nez Perce have been acting up of late?" Lester Winston went on. "That's why I let Mr. Gore talk me into hiring him and his men when we ran into them at Fort Bridger. They are worth their fee if they get us safely through to the Payette River Valley." He stopped. "Have you ever been there?"

"No," Fargo said. The Payette River, yes, but not a valley named after the river. Which in itself was peculiar, given how many times he had been through this region.

"Mr. Gore says the soil is so rich, our crops will practically grow themselves. And game is so plentiful we won't ever lack for meat." Lester gazed to the northwest, his eye lit with the gleam of land hunger.

"We were on our way to Oregon Country, but after hearing Mr. Gore talk about how grand the Payette River Valley is, we changed our minds."

"This Gore must be some talker," Fargo said, and noticed that it caused Rinson to frown.

"He does have a silver tongue," Lester said. "But he's a fine gentleman. The salt of the earth, if you ask me."

"I haven't met many of those," Fargo said drily.

Rinson let out a small hiss of annoyance. "Are we going to sit here jawing all day, Winston? Gore left me to watch over you while he's gone, and I can't say as I like you telling this stranger all there is to know about us. For all we know, he's an outlaw."

"He doesn't look like one."

"Listen to yourself. You can't tell if a person is good or bad by how they look. I say we send him on his way. And if he won't go, we prod him to move him along."

"I don't prod easy," Fargo said.

"Did you hear him?" Rinson asked Lester. "He's not all that friendly. It's best if we're shed of him."

The wagons had stopped. Men, women, and children were all staring with keen interest. They were so far north of the Snake River, in country so rugged and remote, that to run across another white was rare.

One woman in particular caught Fargo's eye. She was young and shapely and wore a bright blue bonnet that complemented her darker blue dress. From under the bonnet, fine yellow hair cascaded, shimmering like gold in the sunlight. Fargo couldn't tell much else about her from that distance, but what he could tell prompted him to say to Lester Winston, "I'd like to ride with you awhile. Maybe share your supper."

Rinson growled, "Like hell."

Now it was Lester Winston who frowned. "Need I remind you that I am the leader of this wagon train? I'll make the decision, not you."

"Gore won't like it."

"He's not here. And while I'll admit that our safety should be uppermost on our minds, I refuse to think the worst of everyone we meet. We must all be Good Samaritans, Mr. Rinson."

"Good what?"

"Haven't you read the Bible?" Lester asked. "The milk of human kindness separates us from the beasts, and we must never let the flow run dry."

"I'm not all that fond of milk," Rinson said. "And I never learned to read nor write."

Winston turned to Fargo. "Yes, by all means, come join us. My Martha won't mind feeding you. And it will be nice to have someone new to talk to."

"Damn it," Rinson fumed. To Fargo he said, "Mister, you have no idea what you are letting yourself in for. Victor Gore is liable to have you stomped into the dirt, and that's no lie."

"I don't stomp easy, either," Fargo said, and gigged the Ovaro. He had the feeling he was about to poke his head into a bear trap, and if he wasn't careful, the steel jaws would snap his head right off.

No other series packs this much heat!

THE TRAILSMAN

**Follow the trail of the gun-slinging heroes of
Penguin's Action Westerns at
penguin.com/actionwesterns**